Iwein

Also published by the University of Nebraska Press

Hartmann von Aue, *Erec,* translated with an introduction by J. W. Thomas

Wirnt von Grafenberg, *Wigalois: The Knight of Fortune's Wheel,* translated with an introduction by J. W. Thomas

Eilhart von Oberge, *Tristant,* translated with an introduction by J. W. Thomas

Iwein

by

HARTMANN VON AUE

TRANSLATED, WITH AN INTRODUCTION, BY
J. W. Thomas

UNIVERSITY OF NEBRASKA PRESS

LINCOLN AND LONDON

Library of Congress Cataloging in Publication Data

Hartmann von Aue, 12th cent.
  Iwein.

  Includes bibliographical references.
  I. Title.
PT1534.I3 1979   831'.2   79–1139
ISBN: 0-8032-7331-2

First Printing: 1979
Second Printing: 1984

To my esteemed colleague
Norman H. Binger
on the occasion of his retirement

CONTENTS

PREFACE

Few stories were as widely known during the Middle Ages as the account of Iwein and Laudine, which appeared in French, Welsh, English, Norse, Swedish, Danish, Icelandic, and two German variants. The older German version, that by the Swabian nobleman Hartmann von Aue, won instant popularity and became a model of form, style, and language for the many courtly epics which his countrymen composed up to the beginning of the modern period. In recent years, his *Iwein* has enjoyed a remarkable revival among medieval scholars as traditional interpretations have been challenged by new ones. Contemporary critics, although disagreeing with each other on many aspects of the work, are united in maintaining that it deserves a much higher rank as a piece of literature than their immediate predecessors gave it.

This first English translation of Hartmann's verse novel has been prepared in the belief that it will be useful to scholars who do not read Middle High German easily and that it will also be of interest to laymen. I would like to express my gratitude to Vivian MacQuown, Robin Barnard, and Andrea Bryant, of the University of Kentucky Library, for locating and making available the extensive literature on *Iwein*.

INTRODUCTION

Hartmann's Works, Sources, and Reception

Hartman von Aue was one of four great epic poets writing at the end of the twelfth and the beginning of the thirteenth centuries who ushered in the Hohenstaufen renaissance in Germany and dominated longer narrative literature there for over two centuries. Since he appears in no official document of his time, our knowledge of Hartmann is limited to what can be derived from personal comments in his works, brief references to him in the works of other medieval writers, two manuscript illustrations which give him an identifiable coat of arms, and certain linguistic peculiarities. On the basis of this rather scanty evidence, he appears to have been a well-educated knight of the servant nobility who took part in a crusade, composed a considerable amount of lyric and epic verse between 1180 and 1203, died sometime after 1210 and before 1220, and was native to the northern part of what is now the canton of Zurich, in Switzerland. The designation *von Aue* does not tell exactly where, since there are several places with this name in the region, but most scholars have favored either the Rhine town of Eglisau or the Lake Zelle island of Reichenau, whose monastic school the poet may have attended as a lay student.[1]

The works of Hartmann reveal a greater variety than those of any other German poet of his day. He composed a long, didactic lover's plaint, *Die Klage* (The Lament); two Arthurian verse novels, *Erec* and *Iwein*; a church legend with a courtly setting, *Gregorius*; a courtly novella with a religious theme, *Der arme Heinrich* (Poor Henry); and sixteen songs, which can be divided into three groups: courtly love songs, songs renouncing courtly love or worldly pleasures, and crusade songs. Since Hartmann constantly improved his poetic expression—by reducing or eliminating archaic words, words of strictly regional usage, dual forms of words, and awkward structures to achieve a rhyme—it is possible to establish a fairly reliable relative chronology of his writings by examining the language. Most contemporary scholars accept this order: *Die Klage*, the courtly love songs, *Erec*, *Gregorius*, the renunciation and crusade songs, *Der arme Heinrich*, and *Iwein*.[2] Each of the longer works, except the last, was the first of its kind in German literature.

Die Klage is a poem of 1,914 verses, the purpose of which is to propound the doctrine of courtly love. Using the form of the Latin *altercatio*, it presents an argument between the heart and the body, in which the body bewails the loss of all happiness because of courtly love and the heart tells of the exertions and self-denial necessary for the true service of courtly love, an activity rewarded by the *summum bonum* of knightly life: the love of God and the esteem of men. The two disputants come to an agreement, and the body goes off to represent the heart with its lady love. Although many of the ideas expressed in the work were new to German letters, all were a part of an affected and elaborate dialectic which had developed during the twelfth century in the songs of Provençal troubadors. Indeed, it is quite likely that Hartmann modeled his poem after some lost Romance composition. In *Die Klage* the author reveals two characteristics which appear in his subsequent major writings: a strongly didactic tendency and a judicious approach to his subject. What is less typical here is that he treats purely literary conceits which had no real connection with the life of Hartmann's time, courtly or otherwise. This is also true in his early lyric verse.

Although several of Hartmann's contemporaries, notably Heinrich von Morungen and Reinmar von Hagenau, could breathe new life into the restricted content and stylized expression characteristic of the courtly love song as it entered

Germany from France, he could not. Heinrich had passion and fire, Reinmar could convey fine nuances of sorrow and pain, but Hartmann's chief talents—clarity and a rationality which tended to moralize—could not give spirit to empty conventions, to a social game. In his courtly love songs, neither the joys nor the sorrows which the singer gains from his relationship to the highborn lady are convincing, and his extreme devotion is uninteresting.

Hartmann's expository and early lyric verse demonstrate mastery of language and form, but he apparently did not find their subject matter really compatible. So it is perhaps no accident that his first epic work should stress the danger inherent in the complete devotion to the noble lady of the courtly love songs. His source was Chretien de Troyes's *Erec*, the earliest Arthurian romance. Hartmann's version is considerably longer; however, the basic plot remains unchanged. Erec, a young knight of Arthur's court, is insulted by an unknown, armed knight whom he cannot challenge because he is not dressed for combat. He follows the stranger and the next day borrows spear and armor, defeats his antagonist, and wins a bride, Enite. The young couple go to Arthur's court, where they receive an enthusiastic welcome, and then, after an elaborate wedding and a colorful tournament (in which Erec greatly distinguishes himself), journey to the hero's native land. When his father, the king, turns over the rule of the country to him, Erec and Enite reach a pinnacle of success and happiness. Unfortunately, the hero is so dominated by physical desire for his wife that he devotes himself completely to his love and gives up all other pursuits. One day he is shocked and angered to find that he has lost his reputation as a knight and, so he mistakenly thinks, also the respect of his wife. Taking Enite with him, Erec sets out on a long and dangerous journey, during which he frequently must defend himself against enemies. When he has re-established his fame and his wife has proven her loyalty, they return to Arthur's court and remain there as highly honored guests until the death of Erec's father. Chretien ends the story here, with the hero being crowned by Arthur as a vassal king amid great pomp and pageantry. In

Hartmann's account, Erec is Arthur's peer. He goes back to his country, is crowned, and rules the land for many years as a wise, God-fearing monarch. His love for Enite is not diminished, but it is more restrained.

The French tale effectively exploits the excitement of combat and extravagant festivities and is certainly the more dramatic of the two. The German work is more reflective, and its ending presents a significant departure from Chrétien's romance of adventure and Arthurian manners. Not only is Arthur reduced to being a king among kings, but the importance of his court as an arbiter of values and customs is also reduced. It is less important that Erec is praised and feted in Arthur's land than that he is warmly received in his own. It is also less significant that he has acquired the balance between love of brave deeds and the love of a lady expected of a model knight than that he has learned, through pain and hardship, how to be a successful monarch. With Hartmann, education was a practical, not an aesthetic, matter.

The didactic tendency which is occasionally evident in Hartmann's *Erec* is much more pronounced in *Gregorius*, which was based on the *Vie du pape Grégoire*.[3] The theme of the German work is that a man can forsake the role which God has chosen for him only at the risk of ruining his life and losing his soul. The hero is born as the result of an incestuous relationship between a young king and his sister and is brought up by a fisherman and his wife under the direction of an abbot who is preparing the child for the priesthood. At fourteen the boy discovers that his parents belonged to the nobility—although he does not learn who they were—and decides to give up his study and become a knight. He does this in spite of the repeated warnings of the abbot and in spite of a document written by his mother in which she confessed to the incest and expressed the hope that her child would devote his life to God and to doing penance for the sins of his parents. The boy sets out and, by chance, comes to his native land (which his mother rules), frees it from invaders, and marries its queen. When he discovers their relationship, he is so overcome by guilt that, as penance, he chains himself to a rock in the wilderness, where he remains for seventeen years. At the end of this time, the pope dies; two of those who are to select a successor are told in a vision that it should be Gregorius, whom they find and bring to Rome. He is elected and becomes a great leader of the Church. Thus, the hero fulfills his destiny, but only after sin, despair, and many years of great suffering.

The practicality underlying the Arthurian adventures of *Erec* and the religious spirit of *Gregorius* also distinguish the lyric verse which followed these works. One song, which forgoes the service of a highborn lady, has, in addition to its humor, a serious purpose: to replace a romantic fiction with a meaningful relationship, while the other renunciation songs and the crusade songs turn away from secular and temporal values and advocate the love and service of God. These poems, unlike the earlier ones, are quite original and give the impression of sincerity.

In *Der arme Heinrich* Hartmann presents a version of the Job story in which the hero at first fails God's testing. Heinrich von Aue is a nobleman who apparently has all one could desire: wealth, power, and every favorable attribute of body, mind, and spirit. But he is self-righteous and accepts his good fortune as a just desert rather than as a gift of God. When he is stricken with leprosy, his former piety is seen to have been no more than a social convention as he rails intransigently against his fate. Doctors of the most famous medical centers tell him that he can be cured only by heart's blood freely given by a pure maiden. In despair, Heinrich withdraws from society to the farm of a loyal tenant, whose daughter eventually learns of the remedy and insists on sacrificing herself. Nobleman and girl journey to Salerno, where a physician is to take the blood from her heart. However, at the last moment, when she is on the operating table, the hero cannot bring himself to gain health at such a price, and the two return home. On the way, God rewards Heinrich's unselfishness and his willingness to accept his lot with a miracle, and he is cured. Heinrich marries the farmer's daughter, they have a long and happy life, and they enter at last into God's kingdom.

Thanks to Thomas Mann's *Der Erwählte* (English title: *The Holy Sinner*) and the various modern treatments of Hartmann's novella in ballad, verse epic, opera, short story, and drama, the contents of *Gregorius* and *Der arme Heinrich* have become well known to today's public. In the thirteenth century, however, *Iwein* was much more popular, as demonstrated by the frequency of medieval references to it and by the relatively large number of extant manuscripts—twenty-eight—in which it appears. This, Hartmann's last work, is obviously based chiefly or entirely on Chrétien's romance, *Yvain, le chevalier au lion*, but the Frenchman's sources are more problematical. There was a historical Owein, son of King Urien of Rheged (an area of Northern England), who fought against Saxons in the sixth century, was celebrated in song as a Celtic hero, and was linked to King Arthur by Geoffrey of Monmouth in his *Historia Regum Britanniae*. However, the scanty information about him which has been preserved shows no relationship to the events of the romance, and the antecedents of its separate incidents have been sought by some in classical literature and mythology and by others in Celtic folksongs and folktales. One school of thought makes the French author the sole creator of the story, while another maintains that he drew his material almost entirely from older tales or perhaps even a single tale.[4]

The question of Chrétien's sources is closely tied to the nature of the connection between *Yvain* and the Welsh Mabinogi *Owein*, which presents a ruder version of essentially the same story. Although each has been given priority by different scholars, the majority opinion seems to be that both drew from the same tale or tales, but that the Welsh writer also knew the French work. The six other medieval treatments of this story are based directly or indirectly on *Yvain*. King Hákon the Old (1217–63) had it rendered into Old Norse prose as *Ívens Saga*, the original of which was lost but which is still extant in a shortened Icelandic version. And Queen Eufemia, wife of King Hákon Magnússon, commissioned a Swedish translation, known as *Herra Ivan Lejonriddaren* (ca. 1303), which apparently was based on both *Ívens Saga* and *Yvain*.[5] The Swedish work, in turn, was the source of one in Danish. The Middle English romance, *Iwain and Gawain*, comes directly from the French, although in an abridged form, while Ulrich Füetrer's *Iban*, a German adaptation of the late fifteenth century, derives primarily from Hartmann's *Iwein*.[6]

Although Hartmann twice mentions his habit of reading,

little sign of it appears in his works. *Erec* contains literary references which point to Ovid's *Metamorphoses*, Lucan's *Pharsalia*, and Horace's *Ars Poetica*, and there is an allusion to an episode concerning Aeneas which is in neither Hartmann's source nor Heinrich von Veldeke's *Eneit* (ca. 1183) and might indicate that he knew Vergil's work. No clear evidence exists of any knowledge of French narratives beyond *Pape Grégoire* and Chétien's *Erec, Yvain*, and possibly *Lancelot*, and there is no mention or obvious influence of any German epic literature, although it has been assumed that Hartmann was familiar with *Eneit*, Lamprecht's *Alexander*, and the *Rolandslied*.[7] The traditional nature of his lyric verse, however, in itself implies a broad contact with Romance and German courtly love songs, which he probably heard rather than read. Moreover, one of his early songs has a meter and a rhyme scheme which were borrowed from the French trouvère Gace Brulé.[8]

Certainly one reason for Hartmann's writings being unaffected by the German narrative writing of his time was its lack of originality and sophistication: it offered no grist for his mill, and he had to look abroad and within. However, he himself exerted a strong influence, not only on the writers of his day, but on many others of the following generations. An editor of Hartmann has stated that no other German poet of the Middle Ages came close to having as great an inspirational and molding effect on contemporaries and posterity as he and has maintained that most subsequent medieval German literature was dominated by his style and language.[9] It is certainly true that his works quickly became models of style, language, and form for all those poets who aspired to compose courtly epic verse for the growing audience of affluent nobility. Especially his *Iwein* served as an example of a work which was free of everything awkward, coarse, and regional.

The first of his contemporaries to show Hartmann's influence was his fellow Swiss, Ulrich von Zazikhoven, whose *Lanzelet* (composed after *Erec* and before *Iwein*) is more courtly in language than in content, even though its hero is a well-known Arthurian knight. The next was Wirnt von Grafenberg, who was familiar with both *Erec* and *Iwein* and showed, in his *Wigalois*, mastery of the new lucid and elevated speech, as well as of what had already become a characteristic epic structure.[10] By the time Gottfried von Strassburg's *Tristan and Isold* appeared, some seven years after *Iwein*, Hartmann's reputation, particularly as a stylist, was firmly established. Since no medieval writer was as competent as Gottfried to judge Hartmann's specific talents, it is worthwhile to note how he does so. "Hartmann von Owe," he wrote in his famous literary digression, "how he adorns his stories inside and out with words and wisdom! How his language strikes the true meaning of the tale! How clear and splendid his crystalline speech is and always will be! It approaches one with decorum, comes near and pleases the well-mannered spirit. Whoever can rightly appreciate fine expression must grant the man of Owe the crown and the laurels."[11] Gottfried goes on to contrast such language very favorably with what he considered the obscurity of Wolfram von Eschenbach and to imply that the writings of his two most famous contemporaries were quite different. In many respects they were, but they shared a pronounced moral and social commitment. Wolfram speaks of Hartmann as the creator of the German Arthurian novel and looked more deeply into *Iwein* in particular than many of its modern critics have done. It is probably due largely to this work that his *Parzival* portrays Arthurian society, not as a chivalric ideal, but as an imperfect, self-centered stage in individual and social development.

Other contemporaries thought to have been influenced by Hartmann are the lyric poets Reinmar von Hagenau and Walther von der Vogelweide and the anonymous author of the *Nibelungenlied*.[12] Among the many later medieval poets who, through borrowing or by direct reference, showed their familiarity with Hartmann, those who wrote courtly novels are most prominent, but authors of heroic narratives, verse tales, and love songs are also included. That artists knew his work is witnessed by the survival of murals depicting scenes from *Iwein*.[13]

The Theme of *Iwein*

Although the central idea of *Iwein* should be obvious, the work has been misunderstood by all scholars up to the present generation, and, even now, there is no clear agreement on what it is about. This question, more than any other, has provoked a rapidly increasing interest in Hartmann's last composition. For many years it was considered to be merely a complement to *Erec* in which the hero's trials add up only to the teaching that a knight of Arthurian romance should find a balance between his dedication to jousting and his devotion to a lady. Since this opinion still has some defenders and its opponents are divided, the theme of *Iwein* will be discussed in detail.[14]

The plot follows that of *Yvain* quite closely, even though more than one-fourth of the verses are new. The added material smoothes transitions, increases motivation, and generalizes on the action. More important, however, it provides a consistent series of clues to the interpretation of a story which, as Chrétien tells it, is ambiguous. Of particular significance in his respect are the three lines with which Hartmann introduces his version: "He who turns his heart to true kindness [*rehtiu güete*] will have God's favor [*saelde*] and man's esteem [or honor: *êre*]." The audience is thus informed immediately that *Iwein*, like *Die Klage*, *Gregorius*, and *Der arme Heinrich*, will deal with gaining the high regard of God and man and, like *Der arme Heinrich*, will show that the way to this goal leads through true kindness and compassion. This theme is reinforced throughout the work by references to the three values of which it is composed.[15] The narrator supports his opening statement by referring to King Arthur as one who knew how to gain such fame that his name will live forever, and then he begins his tale.

The first scene has nothing to do with *rehtiu güete* or *saelde*, only with *êre*. In a bitter altercation, the seneschal Keii accuses Kalogrenant of trying to gain esteem at the expense of others and the queen of demeaning the Arthurian knights, while Kalogrenant and the queen denounce Keii for his spiteful jealousy when anyone else is honored. The quarrel serves as a background and introduction to the events which Kalogrenant recounts afterward. The nucleus of his story is the definition of *aventiure* (the knightly quest) he gives when he tells the giant herdsman that he is looking for a man in armor to defeat in combat so that people will think more highly of him.[16] The validity of this means of winning esteem is placed in question by all four of the people he meets. The herdsman says that he himself is a friend of everyone who does him no harm, and he obviously cannot understand why the knight should be deliberately searching for trouble. Askalon, the defender of the spring, does not comprehend this either and denounces Kalogrenant for his *hôchvart* (overweening pride) in having destroyed the forest and killed the game without provocation or proper declaration of hostilities. The kindly host implies disapproval when he states that no one has ever before stopped at his castle on such a mission, and he and his daughter show that their regard does not depend on prowess in combat by receiving the returning Kalogrenant—defeated, footsore, and half naked—with as much cordiality and honor as they did when he was mounted and resplendent in armor. Another element has, therefore, been added to the theme of *rehtiu güete*, *saelde*, and *êre*; it is *hôchvart*, the attempt to gain the esteem of men without regard for true kindness or God's favor. In terms of medieval theology, this is *superbia*, a sin for which both Gregorius and Heinrich had to atone.

Iwein declares that he will avenge Kalogrenant, and another dispute involving *êre* ensues, in which the queen now sides with Iwein against Keii. The hero then steals away secretly, "like a man who knew how to win and preserve honor by being clever," because he is afraid that the distinction of representing Arthur's court against the defender of the spring will go to Gawein. In the fierce battle which follows, Askalon is mortally wounded and flees toward his castle, pursued by Iwein, who strikes him again as their horses race through the gate because he is afraid that Keii's ridicule will decrease his *êre* if he cannot prove his victory by killing or capturing Askalon.[17] Imprisoned between the two portcullises, the hero sees the grief of Askalon's subjects at his burial, but he feels no compassion: "he would not have cared a straw if the entire court had died and was lying here on biers." However, when Laudine, in great sorrow, tears her clothing and exposes some of her bare flesh, its beauty so inflames Iwein's passion that, for a moment, he forgets his concern for his *êre*. He quickly wins the widow of the man he has slain and becomes the new ruler of the land and defender of the spring.

Arthur arrives, disturbs the spring, and designates Keii to represent him. Iwein easily defeats the seneschal, ridiculing him as he lies prostrate.[18] After the Arthurian court has been festively entertained and is about to depart, Gawein persuades the hero that he could lose his reputation as a valiant knight if he were to settle down at once, so Iwein tricks Laudine into permitting him to be gone for a year. He and Gawein take part in a succession of tournaments in which he is so successful and gains such fame that he forgets his solemn oath to return on time. Lunete appears before the court of Arthur to denounce Iwein for his disloyalty and to proclaim that Laudine is repudiating him. Crushed by the public rebuke (an attack on his *êre)* and the loss of lands, property, and wife, Iwein loses his mind and flees to the wilderness, where he lives as a naked wild man.

The traditional view of Iwein has been that he was a model knight whose only flaw was a passion for jousting and whose only offense was overstaying his leave. But, even though the narrator condemns him just once, the plain facts of the story reveal a young man who, without provocation, invades another's land, destroys his property, and kills him. No compassion moves the intruder when he hears the victim's subjects mourning his death, and no sense of propriety restrains him from wooing and marrying the widow only two days after the funeral. He then defeats and ridicules a fellow knight of Arthur's court (his opponent might well have been his friend Gawein, whom he had wished to deprive of a victory by being the first to arrive at the spring). He tricks his wife into letting him leave her and the land defenseless for a year, so that he may gain more fame, and then fails to return by the promised date. It is clear that his obsession with *êre* has caused him to fall prey to *superbia*.[19] The hero is, in fact, more depraved than either Gregorius or Heinrich, and we can expect that the expiation of his sin will be long and difficult. However, we can be hopeful of his eventual redemption for two reasons: one is that he apparently really loves Laudine, the other is that he is not completely without compassion. Indeed, years before, he had been the only knight at Arthur's court to speak to Lunete after she had committed some unstated infraction of etiquette.[20]

Hartmann's account of Iwein's insanity is somewhat longer than that of Chrétien because the German was more intent on emphasizing both the degree and the appropriateness of the punishment for the hero's *superbia*: the knight who would do anything to gain the esteem of men has become a naked wild man, blackened by the elements, who lives on a most primitive level. The selfishness which had characterized all his actions is strikingly contrasted with the *güete* of the girl who finds him and has such compassion that she weeps bitterly on seeing his degradation, persuades her lady to help him, and later—at the risk of her life—uses up an entire box of magic ointment to cure him. And so selfless is her kindness that she takes care that Iwein should not know of her assistance or even that she had seen him in a wretched state.

The hero's monologue when he regains his sanity is the most important addition which Hartmann makes to Chrétien's plot. In the long discourse on his former life, which Iwein believes to be a dream, the key word is *êre* (appearing five times as noun and verb) and the emphasis is on the contrast between the splendor of the dream and the bleakness of reality. The audience, however, has been prepared to see more deeply into the hero's situation and associates his concept of *êre* with the delusion and lack of substance of a dream. When Iwein recalls that in the dream he had won a rich land and a wife in battle through his own strength alone, the audience cannot fail to compare this *superbia* with the *rehtiu güete* of the opening verse. The monologue demonstrates that there has been no sudden and complete conversion of the hero, but, as he makes a new start, his doubts about the reality of his past life stimulate a gradual reexamination of his past values.[21]

In the series of events which follows, Iwein does penance for having abandoned his wife by protecting a succession of other women and atones for his act of violence by preventing others from perpetrating similar crimes. The first episode shows a marked resemblance to the hero's encounter with Askalon and Laudine. The arrogant Count Aliers has laid waste the country of the lady of Narison (as Iwein had done to Askalon's), presumably to force her to marry him and to give him control of her land.[22] Iwein leads an army which defeats the invaders and then pursues the count up to the gate of his castle, where he takes the count prisoner in proper knightly fashion. The hero could hardly have missed the parallel between the actions and goals of Aliers and his own in the earlier scene, a recognition which may have encouraged him to treat the count with consideration. Although this incident does not show that Iwein's heart has been turned to *rehtiu güete,* it does demonstrate that he is no longer obsessed with self-aggrandizement and can be considerate toward others, both friends and foes. We are, therefore, prepared for his first deed of compassion—the rescue of the lion—which follows soon after he leaves the Lady of Narison. And when, contrary to Iwein's fears, the lion does not attack him but is grateful and becomes his faithful companion and protector, it is apparent that true kindness may indeed win him God's favor.

The two arrive by chance at the spring, and the memory of his former happiness moves Iwein to despair at the loss of wife, land, and *êre*. At first he is completely taken up with sorrow and self-pity, but several things happen which point him in the direction of *rehtiu güete*. When he falls to the ground in a faint, the lion believes him dead and starts to kill itself from grief, thus giving him an example of devotion and selflessness. Soon afterwards, the condemned Lunete first convinces him that his situation is by no means as desperate as hers and then lets him see that others, as well as he, suffer from his mistakes. Finally, when she declines to risk his life to save her own, he sees an instance of real altruism. However, Iwein's plan to kill himself in front of Laudine, as soon as he has defeated Lunete's accusers, shows that he is still an egoist who has not yet overcome his *superbia*. He grieves for his losses rather than for his misdeeds.

The most important, though not the last, station in Iwein's moral pilgrimage is the sojourn at the castle of Gawein's brother-in-law. It begins, like the previous episode, with an example of unselfishness, as the hero's host and the entire court strive to conceal their anguish so that they will not cause him distress. But Iwein shows that he has learned from the lion and from Lunete, for, where he had doubted the seriousness of her trouble compared to his, he now notices the sorrow of those around him, asks about its cause, and feels compassion for them, even before he hears of their connection to his friend. The hero not only is willing to help but also states that it is his duty to do so if this does not interfere with his promise to champion Lunete. The reasons Iwein gives his host for the decision are pertinent to the theme of the work in that they represent three progressive steps in the direction of *rehtiu güete*. He says he will fight the giant Harpin for the sake of his host, for the sake of his hostess (Gawein's sister), and because they are innocent victims. That is, he

will aid them as a result of a purely personal relationship, out of
consideration for a friend, and because of a disinterested obligation to protect the innocent against ruthless aggression.
Iwein will not allow his hostess to fall on her knees in thanks before him, saying, with the first indications of humility, that it
would be far too great an * êre* for such an unimportant man as
himself to have Sir Gawein's sister at his feet.

When the hero goes to mass as a part of his preparation for the
battle, thus showing a readiness to accept divine assistance, we
see a further indication that he is conquering his inordinate desire for the honor of men. But when Harpin does not appear,
Iwein must decide whether to save Lunete or Gawein's relatives, and it becomes apparent that the possibility of dishonor
before men is still of great concern to him. Hartmann shows
keen perception in the portrayal of the hero's painful dilemma
as he weighs not only matters of pride (the relative injury to his
reputation of one decision as opposed to another) but also the
question of morality. He does not know whether his primary
commitment to Lunete, his debt to her for saving his life, and
the fact that he is to blame for her desperate situation should
take precedence over his friendship for Gawein, or whether the
welfare of an entire family should be considered of greater value
than the life of a single individual. And all the while he is tor-
tured by fears that he will lose the last of society's respect for
him if he abandons either. It is significant that just at this difficult time the author should echo his opening lines by having the
pleading host remind Iwein that God grants His favor and the
esteem of men to him who is compassionate. The hero, for his
part, turns to God with a prayer that he may do what is right.
Soon afterwards, the giant rides up to the gate and the problem
is solved.

We are struck by the modesty of Iwein as he prepares for battle. He believes that God will bring down his opponent and that
he will be strengthened by the justice of his host's cause and the
hôchvart of the enemy. This word, first used by Askalon to casti-
gate the one who brought violence to his land, indicates that the
hero again sees his own past in an aggressor. He makes the impression stronger when he goes on to say that he himself is in no
position to censure any knight. Indeed, Harpin's crimes are similar to those of the hero. Where Iwein had committed murder on

the way to a marriage which brought him increased wealth and esteem, the giant had resorted to murder when such a marriage was denied him. And Harpin's attempts to humiliate those who had exposed him to ridicule differ only in degree, not in kind, from Iwein's treatment of Keii. The resemblances, however, only emphasize the hero's progress from *superbia* toward *rehtiu güete*. Again declaring his confidence that God will support the right, he attacks the giant and, with timely aid from the lion, kills him. When he then identifies himself only as "the knight with the lion," it is not just a refusal to accept, under his own name, the esteem of men for his act but also an open declaration that he could not have accomplished it unassisted.

Although Iwein is still concerned with his personal *êre* as he hurries off to rescue Lunete, it later becomes clear that he is motivated chiefly by compassion and an objective regard for justice. When he catches sight of Lunete by the pyre, he is pained by her shame and distress and is confident that God, her innocence, and the lion will enable him to free her. In response to the lord high steward's warning that he will have three opponents, the hero replies that he will also have two allies: God and truth. There is now no trace of the boastful, egocentric attitude which he displayed the first time he entered Laudine's land. And, in the battle which follows, it is not his own wounds, but those of the lion, that incite him to the supreme effort which brings victory.

The humility which Iwein has learned prevents him from disclosing his identity to Laudine after the trial by combat, even though he loves her and hopes eventually to be reunited with her. The egoistical plan of public suicide has, of course, been forgotten. As the two part, the theme of *rehtiu güete, saelde,* and *êre* appears once more in their farewells. "God protect you," says the hero, "and give you His favor and the esteem of men." "I commend you to God," she replies. "May He in His kindness soon transform your sorrow to happiness and honor." Iwein departs, but soon the lion can walk no farther, and its tender-hearted master lifts it onto the horse. At last the badly injured pair arrive at a castle whose compassionate lord receives them hospitably and has his two beautiful daughters treat and bind their wounds. It is noteworthy that they have not only great healing skill but also *güete*.

The arrival at this place, the dominant characteristic of which is friendly concern for others, is truly symbolic, for one can see that Iwein, too, has turned his heart to true kindness. This is confirmed when, after convalescing, knight and lion travel on and are overtaken by the girl messenger of the younger Countess of Black Thorn, who tells him she has come a long distance to ask him a favor. "It is not a matter of favors," he replies, "I shall not refuse help to any good person who really needs it," and notices with sympathy that she has suffered hardships on the way. The hero's offer to champion Lunete came primarily from a sense of personal gratitude and guilt, for she had saved his life and he was responsible for her having been condemned, and his offer to fight for Gawein's relatives was due, at least in part, to their connection with his friend. But now he is ready to aid any good person in need, without considering the risks, and he does not consider such help a favor, but simply a duty. This is indeed *rehtiu güete*, and the narrator now has only to disclose how *saelde* and *êre* follow.

With respect to the theme of the story, the most striking feature about the adventure of the two giants is the revelation of the character modification which accompanies the loss of *superbia*. Reviled by the townspeople below the castle, Iwein does not respond in great anger (as Chrétien's hero does), but tries to convince them that he wishes to be their friend. He likewise refuses to take offense at the even more abusive language of the watchman and does not lose his composure or genial manner either when his host scorns him as a coward before the battle or when he threatens him angrily afterwards. The hero attends mass on the morning of his ordeal and, at its conclusion, does not (like Yvain) gain permission to leave by a false promise to return, but simply tells the truth. The contrast between Iwein's present cordial equanimity and his former rashness, sensitivity to criticism, and petty vindictiveness graphically illustrates how a personality can be perverted by egoism and overconcern for the esteem of men. The hero continues to show his compassion by sparing the life of one of the giants, as well as by his sympathy for the miserable plight of the three hunded maidens. That the latter should gain their freedom as a result of Iwein's ordeal and subsequent intercession is an indication that he has completed his atonement and has received God's favor. This is implied by the prayer of the departing maidens as they urgently beseech God—in the words of Hartmann's theme—to grant their benefactor *saelde, êre*, a long life, and paradise thereafter.

Iwein's return to Arthur's court invites comparison between his present and former personality traits. When he and Gawein use up their spears during the trial by combat and resort to their swords, they dismount so their steeds will not be injured. The narrator applauds this consideration for animals, and we remember that it did not appear in the battle between Iwein and Askalon. Of greater importance in revealing the hero's development, however, is the fact that it was he who initiated the conversation which led to the revelation of his and Gawein's identity, for such an act could easily have been interpreted as cowardice. Iwein was also the first to insist that he had lost the battle and that his opponent had won. Although the audience might have protested that, as the representative of a wronged client, he had no right to do this, it does afford Hartmann an opportunity to show a marked change in his hero: the knight who once killed a fleeing man to gain proof of victory now insists at length that he has been conquered. Still, he has not been, and his exploits in the conflict, together with his identification as the "Knight with the Lion," greatly increase his *êre*.

It was loss of honor and land, as well as the loss of his wife, which caused Iwein to steal from Arthur's court in despair after Lunete's denunciation, but it is love that draws him away and back to Laudine in the final episode. With complete humility, he confesses his error and asks forgiveness, and they are reconciled. The hero has turned his heart toward true kindness and, therefore, at last receives both God's favor and the esteem of men as a reward.

Hartmann's theme is illustrated in the lives of other characters as well as in that of his hero. We first meet Laudine when she is tearing her clothing and raging with grief at the death of her husband, behavior which seems natural and even commendable until she turns her wrath on God, accusing him of complicity in the death. This *superbia* certainly could not be justified by the pious Hartmann and is doubtless intended as a warning to the audience that the lady's subsequent deportment might be less than exemplary. This intimation is reinforced by the action of her close confidante, who ventures to approach her the same day with arguments that she remarry. Lunete's reasons—the possible loss of spring, land, and esteem—indicate at once that Laudine's weakness is the same as Iwein's, an obsession with *ère*. She then tells of the impending arrival of Arthur and the damage to her mistress's reputation if she has no one to defend the spring, but she does not insist that the king will actually seize the land. The girl repeatedly stresses the matter of *ère*, and her efforts are soon successful. It is true that the narrator seems to defend Laudine against inconstancy; however, his comments are ironic, as is the prevailing tone of the episode as it is related in *Yvain*.[23] When Hartmann composed the passage, he certainly would have mentally compared her vacillation and early capitulation with the uncompromising devotion of Enite in a similar situation, and he would have remembered that Lunete's arguments are the same as those which caused the mother of Gregorius to enter into the fatal marriage with her son.

As soon as Laudine is convinced that the knight who killed her husband must have been greater than he (and, therefore, better able to preserve her honor), she makes excuses for the stranger, telling herself that he had acted only out of self-defense. Now she needs simply to be reassured that he has such standing that the world will not criticize her for accepting the slayer of her husband. When she learns that the stranger is Iwein, the son of King Urien, she agrees at once to marry him and cannot disguise her impatience at any delay, insisting that he be brought to her immediately.[24] Her chief justification for remarrying, the welfare of her people, is shown to be a sophism by the narrator's remark that she would have married him whether her subjects liked it or not. Her real reasons are to maintain her throne and be known abroad as a person of consequence. The satirical comment with which the narrator introduces the wedding festivities condemns both Laudine and Iwein: "The dead man was forgotten as the living one took over honors and land: all became his. A greater celebration was never held in that country before or since."[25] Arthur arrives, his champion is defeated, and he shows his regard for the victor by a state visit. "For the first time she became truly fond of her husband," says the narrator about the bride. "When she had the honor of meeting the king because of him, she saw clearly that she had been lucky."

At Gawein's instigation, Iwein asks his wife for permission to be absent a year, which she reluctantly grants, reminding him that their *êre* and their land will be endangered if he does not return on time.[26] He does not, and Lunete denounces the hero before Arthur's court in language which reveals that it is primarily Laudine's pride which has suffered by Iwein's failure to appear on the date agreed. Neither the medieval audience nor the modern reader could blame her for her anger, but both would feel that a woman who could forget a husband in a single day deserves to be forgotten by his successor.

During Laudine's conversation with the unknown knight who has defended Lunete, she seems less imperious and more sympathetic than she did earlier. She not only notices his wounds, but also asks him to stay with her until they are healed. In response to his statement that he will never stop anywhere until he has gained the favor of his lady, she says that the lady is not wise to reject such a brave man unless he has caused her much grief, thus revealing her own suffering. She betrays a little of her old preoccupation with *êre* by protesting that she could never bear the shame if someone were to see him leaving her land so badly wounded. But an indication that she too is moving toward *rehtiu güete* appears in her farewell, which was quoted above. Scholars have interpreted Laudine's failure to recognize her husband in various ways: some to her discredit, some to his.[27] In any case, it simply does not occur to her that a man who would risk his life against great odds with no expectation of either material gain or fame could be Iwein.

In the final episode, Lunete goes to inform her mistress of the arrival of the knight with the lion and finds her alone at prayer, a fact of symbolic importance with regard to her progress in overcoming *superbia*. The impression of increased humility is then strengthened by Laudine's offer to go to the knight, rather than having him brought before her, since she is the petitioner. On learning his identity, her wounded pride comes to the fore as she protests at taking back a husband who has shown no regard

for her. However, after he confesses his error and begs her forgiveness, she recalls their previous discussion and the sad loyalty of the unknown knight to his lady and is overcome with remorse. She asks his pardon for the pain she has caused him and
falls at his feet in supplication: she too has known sorrow and
has learned kindness from it.[28]

Lunete follows the same pattern of development as do hero
and heroine. At the beginning of the story, she considers the esteem of men so important that she forgives Iwein the murder of
her beloved lord and rescues him because he had once shown her
êre while the other Arthurian knights were snubbing her. The
memory of their affront doubtless contributed to Lunete's in-
sistence that her lady take measures to preserve her own honor
against King Arthur's court when it should arrive at the spring.
Later, in denouncing Iwein, she goes beyond the message of her
mistress and reproaches him bitterly for his ingratitude toward
her, Lunete. Her words also express resentment for the damage
his act has done to her prestige as an adviser to Laudine. The
main part of the history of Lunete's guilt and atonement is told
during the conversation with Iwein while she is imprisoned in
the chapel. She says that she had been thinking of her own advantage as well as Laudine's in helping the hero become ruler of
the country. She also relates how her present misfortune was in
part a result of her arrogance: irritated by the attacks of the lord
high steward, she had haughtily asserted that she could find a
man who could defeat the three best warriors at the court. However, her sufferings have taught her compassion, and when
Iwein volunteers to be her champion, she declines to risk his life
to save hers.

On his return from the battle with Harpin, the hero finds Lunete on her knees beside the pyre in prayer. This is not merely
an expression of her fear, but, as with Laudine, a sign that she
has given up egoistical striving for *êre* and is seeking God's
favor.[29] The messenger who is looking for the knight with the
lion arrives there two weeks later and also finds Lunete at
prayer, in the chapel by the spring. And Lunete shows *rehtiu
güete* in her eagerness to help the girl, even though she is a complete stranger. A new spirit appears in Lunete throughout the
rest of the work. She is still the clever schemer, just as Laudine

remains impulsive, but she is much more modest about her ability to advise and, although she doubts that any of her lady's courtiers will defend the spring, she does not speak scornfully of them, as she did before.

The only other character in the story to show change is the younger Countess of Black Thorn. She does not exhibit the degree of overweening pride that causes Iwein to commit murder and makes Laudine and Lunete accomplices after the fact, but her desire for *êre* does impel her to undertake a course of action which almost brings death to a noble knight. Moreover, her hasty threat to solve the property dispute by getting a champion at Arthur's court reveals more than a trace of the *superbia* which is her sister's dominant trait. Still, her guilt is small and her penance relatively light: a short, though difficult, search for the knight with the lion and a temporary illness. The countess's spiritual development is rapid. As soon as it becomes clear that one of the two champions is likely to be killed, she tries to withdraw her suit and stop the contest, declaring that she would rather give all her property to her sister than be responsible for the death of either knight. With this decision, the younger countess triumphs over *superbia* and turns toward *rehtiu güete*.

Among the unregenerate are not only the patent villains—the giants, Laudine's steward, and the older Countess of Black Thorn—but also the Arthurian community.[30] It is true that its king is cited in the opening lines as proof of the story's theme, but the statement is soon found to be ironic, since subsequent events connect him with neither true kindness nor God's favor, but only with an exaggerated regard for the esteem of men. Indeed, it is obvious from the beginning that Iwein's obsession with *êre*, the source of all his troubles, is a fault he shares both with Arthur and with his fellow knights. This society, which is treated in a consistently satirical, often humorous manner, is portrayed as completely egocentric and largely ineffectual in its dealings with the outside world.[31]

Something of the attitude of the narrator toward Arthur and his court is indicated in the first scene. It is a splendid festival, with all sorts of entertainment—dancing, singing, various sports—but the king leaves his guests to care for themselves while he goes off to make love to his wife (for which he is strongly criticized in *Yvain*), his lord high steward falls asleep, Gawein polishes his weapons, and the other prominent knights of the court sit off by themselves, listening to one of their members tell of his adventures. The impression of casual manners is strengthened by the undignified quarrel between Keii, Kalogrenant, and the queen, and a suspicion of moral insensitivity is created by the fact that no one, including King Arthur, objects to Kalogrenant's definition of the knightly quest as a means of gaining fame at another's expense. The suspicion is confirmed when the king takes his court to the spring and disturbs its waters, wantonly destroying forest and animals. The easy defeat of his champion, Keii, whom the narrator (tongue in cheek) had praised as a mighty warrior, is symbolic of the ineptness of the court even in the area in which it takes most pride. No one criticizes the murder of Askalon or the hasty and unseemly marriage of his widow. Instead, Iwein's comrades rejoice at his success, and Gawein, with an amusing description of an uncouth landholder, persuades him to go in search of further fame instead of carrying out his obligation to defend the land.

The hero overstays his leave and is denounced as a liar and traitor by Lunete, who also tells the king that, since he values honor so highly, he should dismiss Iwein. But Arthur once again shows that the morality of his court is not that of the outside world by sending men to look for Iwein and bring him back. Later it becomes apparent that the Arthurian society, though cherishing *êre*, is not inclined toward dangerous exploits to assist outsiders, for Lunete, Gawein's brother-in-law, and the younger Countess of Black Thorn in turn vainly seek a champion at the Round Table. It is significant that Iwein, after saving Gawein's relatives, does not send them to King Arthur to report their rescue, but to Gawein. His deed is, therefore, a tribute to a personal friend, not to the prestige of the court.

One of the largest additions of new material which Hartmann makes to Chrétien's story deals with the abduction of Guinevere by Meljakanz. In *Yvain*, three separate passages with a total of twenty-six lines mention the event only to explain the absence of Gawein when his brother-in-law is looking for him. These are expanded to a tale of two hundred lines, the purpose of which is to expose the *superbia* of the Arthurian court, as seen in its exaggerated concern for the esteem given by men. At the urging of his knights, the king agrees to preserve his reputation for generosity by granting a stranger anything he might request. And, for fear of losing honor, he keeps his promise even when the stranger asks for the queen. So Guinevere, concerned about her own *ère*, is led away. The knights set out in pursuit, not as an effective group, but individually, apparently because no one wants to share the distinction of rescuing her. As a result, the entire Round Table suffers defeat and humiliation, which is not mitigated by Guinevere's later deliverance, since the narrator fails to say how she managed to return. Thus, the court is punished for its lack of *rehtiu güete*.

When the younger Countess of Black Thorn comes to Arthur's court to find a champion, she is unsuccessful—as Lunete and Gawein's brother-in-law were before her. Only Gawein is willing to fight for someone from the outside, and he has already agreed to represent her sister, without any attempt to ascertain who was in the right. Arthur is sympathetic, but since he must maintain his position as a supporter of traditional procedures, he is ineffective in achieving justice until the trial by combat breaks down. The headlong flight of the entire court at the appearance of the lion is, therefore, more than simply a comic interlude. It is dramatic evidence that this society cannot cope with the outside world, and it suggests that the inadequacy is moral as well as physical. Iwein's stealthy departure is not only an affirmation of his love for Laudine, but also a repudiation of the court to which he once belonged.

Looking back over the history of King Arthur's court, one notes that it has done little to gain esteem, even though that is its chief goal. Nor do its members seem particularly estimable. Keii's malice and boasting make him disliked by his fellows, but these traits are not incompatible with the ideals to which they subscribe. He is presented essentially as a caricature of the Arthurian knight, rather than as a contrast figure. Kalogrenant, who journeys forth to gain *ère* by defeating others in battle, is frightened by the monstrous shepherd and his charges, tries to avoid fighting the larger Askalon, and—like Keii—is easily defeated in the two jousts he undertakes. Gawein differs from Kalogrenant in being a brave and competent warrior and from Keii in being modest and generous. Yet his basic values are the same as theirs: he advises Iwein to neglect duty to gain fame, and, as seen in the Black Thorn affair, he regards combat as an obligation to himself rather than as a means to eliminate injustice. Far from being depicted as an ideal society, the court of Arthur represents the state of mind from which the hero must free himself through suffering and compassionate deeds.[32] It is a state of mind which not only does not contribute to the general welfare but may even be injurious to it: the search for fame by the young ruler of the Isle of Virgins brings misery to hundreds of his subjects.

Eilhart von Oberge, in his *Tristrant*, describes a King Arthur who does not hesitate to lie and deceive in order to help a friend, and Chrétien frequently points to defects in the manners of his court, but Hartmann was the first pronounced moralist to make literary use of the Arthurian tradition and was the first to emphasize the fundamental disparity between its exaltation of fame and pleasure and the Christian ideals of *caritas* and *misericordia*. In this respect, his *Iwein* anticipates the *Queste del saint graal* of the following generation. Still, one should not assume that Hartmann was interested primarily in the morality of the Arthurian court. He uses it chiefly as a measure of the hero's progress. Iwein starts out in competition with Keii, whose ridicule drives him to murder; at the end, he shows himself to be superior to both Arthur and Gawein, for he has learned true kindness.

The final verse of *Iwein* is a prayer that God may grant us His grace and the esteem of men. These words refer back to the initial verses and once more stress Hartmann's theme. They also clarify it by pointing out that the *saelde* and *êre* which follow *rehtiu güete* are the gifts of God. Although not previously stated, this is frequently indicated throughout the work by suggestions of divine intervention and guidance. There are 118 references to God in *Iwein*.[33] Many are simply formulaic and of little significance, but others are included with the specific intention of adding a religious dimension to the events. The first of these is the comment, immediately after the hero becomes insane, that God did not completely forsake him, but sent him (through a squire) a bow and arrows, with which he could get food. The next important reference comes when Iwein prays for God's help in deciding whether to save Lunete or Gawein's relatives. As if in response, Harpin appears and the problem is solved. Encouraged by the answer to his prayer, Iwein then tells his host that God will strike down the giant. During his conversation with Laudine after the rescue of Lunete, the hero says that there will be no help for him unless God causes his lady to remember him. Later, when fighting the two giants, he is confident that he will survive if God is merciful, and, when he strikes the decisive blows, the narrator attributes his success to the blessing of God.

Other characters also benefit from divine intervention. The messenger, lost in the forest at night, calls on God for help and at once hears the sound of a horn from a nearby castle. Moreover, God takes care that she turns in the right direction. Soon afterwards, Gawein's brother-in-law tells her that it was God who sent Iwein to save them. These, and many additional passages of a like nature, reinforce Hartmann's theme by lending a religious connotation to the true kindness which Iwein, like Gregorius and Heinrich, finally achieves.

Structure and Motifs

Like many other medieval verse novels, *Iwein* is more dramatic than narrative in nature. It was composed to be performed before an audience by a professional reader and actor, and over half of it is direct discourse. The work resembles a modern comedy, and, like it, stresses incongruity, includes occasional trivialities, accepts a limited amount of the supernatural, and focuses on a universal social or individual folly. Unity of action is achieved, and the central idea is kept in the spotlight, by an arrangement of scenes which, through similarity and contrast, continuously links new developments with the old. The whole may be compared structurally to a five-act play, one in which the boundaries between the acts are not distinctly marked.[34]

The first act is expository and includes a statement of the theme, some personal remarks by the narrator, an introduction to King Arthur and his court (the standard of manners and morality), and Kalogrenant's tale (an example of that standard in action). The second act recounts the rise and fall of the hero in an adventure which closely parallels that of his cousin. Iwein is braver and more skillful with weapons, but the inordinate thirst for fame which brings Kalogrenant's quest to an ignominious end eventually and inevitably also causes Iwein's ruin. The first half of the third act shows how Iwein lived in the wilderness as a wild man, in stark contrast to his former state and appearance. The second half, introduced by his return to sanity and the monologue on his past life as a dream, presents a variation on act 2: a lady-in-waiting saves the hero's life, a country is threatened by an invader, the hero pursues a knight up to the gates of the knight's castle, and the mistress of the land wants to marry him—these elements are the same. The differences are that Iwein does not kill his opponent and is not driven by a desire for wealth and honor into marrying the lady. Instead, he journeys forth and, on a generous impulse that bodes well for his later development, saves a lion from a dragon.

Act 4 is structurally the most interesting. It also falls into two parts which correlate very closely with each other while recalling scenes from acts 1 and 2. By chance, Iwein arrives at the spring again, where his sorrow and remorse remind the reader of his former arrogance there. He finds Lunete a prisoner, her life in danger—just as she had once discovered him between the two portcullises—and promises to be her champion in a trial by combat. In the following scene he is at the castle of Gawein's brother-in-law, who tells him a story (that of Meljakanz and Arthur's court) in which, as in Kalogrenant's tale, excessive pride leads to humiliation—not for a single knight this time, but for an entire court. The next morning Iwein defeats a giant and then hurries back to Lunete, appearing barely in time to keep his promise. After he is victorious in the trial by combat, he talks with Laudine, who, although she does not recognize him, is reluctant to see him leave her land—as she had been in act 2. An interlude then gives the story of the Black Thorn sisters. The second half of the act reveals the same pattern as the first half. The hero meets a girl and promises to be her champion in a trial by combat. He then goes to a castle where he hears a tale (that of the lord of the Island of Maidens) in which excessive pride brings tragedy to three hundred people; he is later entertained by a knight with the same lavish cordiality that he had received from Gawein's brother-in-law. The next morning he fights two giants. After several days he sets out for Arthur's court, arriving just in time to fulfill his pledge to represent the younger Countess of Black Thorn in the trial. The promise to appear at a specific time, which Iwein twice just manages to keep, recalls the promise to Laudine which he broke. The two halves of the act differ mainly in the development of the hero, who is torn between *êre* and compassion in the first part and exhibits only *rehtiu güete* in the second.

The final act is a close variant of the second. As soon as Iwein has recovered from his wounds, he steals away from Arthur's court and rides to the spring. He disturbs the water again, and Lunete for the second time manages a reconciliation between him and Laudine. The act ends as act 1 began, with personal comments by the narrator and a statement of the theme.

The impression of artistic unity produced by the symmetrical patterning of similar and contrasting scenes is strengthened by the use of various motifs. One such motif is Iwein's act of stealing away from Arthur's court. This occurs three times, at significant places in the story: when he first rides to the spring, when he is denounced by Lunete, and when he finally rejoins Laudine. He leaves, therefore, with arrogance, with despair, and with hope, respectively, but there is in each instance also an overtone of escape. After his first secret departure Gawein persuades him to return; and after the second Arthur sends men to look for him. The third departure, although principally motivated by love for Laudine, seems at the same time to be a flight from a society which has become foreign to him. In essence, the hero leaves behind not just the court, but the whole world, of King Arthur and escapes into the world of the author.

A second motif which serves both a structural and a thematic function is the idea of faithfulness *(triuwe)*. It first appears in a negative form, when Askalon accuses Kalogrenant of being treacherous *(triuwelôs)* in destroying his property without cause or warning. The same condemnation would apply, of course, to Iwein, who commits the same offense. The word does not appear again until the denunciation of the hero by Lunete, who uses it, in various forms, eleven times as she berates him for deserting her mistress. However, the narrator speaks of Iwein's faithfulness to Laudine just before Lunete's tirade and again immediately afterwards. He adds that, in part, it was this questioning of his *triuwe* that drove Iwein insane. Later, when the hero fails to marry the Lady of Narison, the narrator's statement gains some support, but not until he sees the lion attempt to kill itself in grief at his presumed death does Iwein comprehend the full meaning of *triuwe*. Sorrowing at the loss of his wife's affection, he says, "This wild lion has shown me that true loyalty is no small thing." Soon afterwards he tells the imprisoned Lunete that he will be her champion. Apparently remembering her accusation, he says, "If I have any loyalty at all, I can't see you harmed when I can prevent it." The next day, as he tries to decide whether to save Gawein's relatives or Lunete, the word *triuwe* enters his thoughts and makes it impossible for him to desert her. The motif appears a last time in the episode of the two giants. The daughter of the hero's host is described in the most extravagant terms as possessing beauty, wealth, and every virtue to such a degree that an angel's head could be turned, yet she cannot shake Iwein's faithfulness to his wife. The implication throughout is that *triuwe* is a necessary step in learning true kindness.

The figure of the lady in distress, common to most Arthurian novels, becomes, in *Iwein*, a motif which is central to all of the later episodes, appearing in the persons of the Lady of Narison, Gawein's niece, Lunete, the three hundred ladies from the Island of Maidens, and the younger Countess of Black Thorn. Each occurrence is a reminder of the offense that was the immediate cause of the hero's downfall, the abandonment of a wife who needed a protector. And the pains he suffers in rescuing the other ladies can be seen as a fitting penance for his crime.

The reverse of the lady-in-distress motif is that of the hospitable host with the beautiful daughter or daughters. We meet him first in Kalogrenant's tale, next as Gawein's brother-in-law, then as the knight who took in the wounded hero and lion after the Lunete combat, and finally as the lord of the castle where the three hundred ladies were detained. The first three hosts are examples of true kindness (in the case of Gawein's brother-in-law, it is suggested that one learns this through suffering and hardship); the fourth is quite obviously less generous than he at first seems. In general, the motif is an affirmation of the existence in society of an unselfish compassion that is not concerned with status or fame. The exception is simply a practical reminder that not everyone who receives you well is without ulterior interests.

The last motifs to be discussed are the madman-fool (*tôr*) and dream (*troum*) motifs. Unlike those previously examined, these motifs are restricted to a single episode, the wilderness experience and the monologue with which it ends. During the approximately one hundred verses that tell of his life in the wilds, the hero is referred to six times as a *tôr*, in a refrainlike manner which suggests that the narrator is emphasizing the double meaning of the word. This suspicion is confirmed later, in the monologue, when Iwein calls himself a *tôr* and certainly does not mean that he considers himself demented. In his soliloquy the hero recalls his life as a highly esteemed knight whose strength had gained him a wife and a rich land and, while doing so, he constantly repeats the word *dream* (fourteen times in eighty-five verses) until it, too, takes on a different meaning. As the listeners remember the degradation to which the hero's passion for *êre* has brought him, they can agree that he has been a fool. And the vanity and transitory nature of his former egocentric life become more apparent with each reiteration that it was a dream.

Narrator, Style, and Symbolism

The differences of opinion concerning the theme of *Iwein* are largely the result of differences of opinion about the nature and function of the narrator. This figure plays an important role in almost all of the courtly novels of medieval Germany, from Eilhart von Oberge's *Tristrant* (between 1170 and 1190) to Hermann von Sachsenheim's *Die Mörin* (1453). Sometimes he does little more than introduce his story and enliven it with occasional humorous interjections, in other works his personality colors the entire narrative, and in certain novels—*Die Mörin* and Ulrich von Liechtenstein's *Frauendienst*—he is the central character. His comments may at times express the views of his creator, although this is not always the case. Indeed, the intrusions of the narrator generally seem more an attempt to construct a part for the actor-reader who is to present the story to an audience than a device through which the author can interpret it for the broader public. The extent of the narrator's participation, as well as the degree of his omniscience, varies greatly from work to work. In most cases he will admit, even flaunt, his limited knowledge, insisting that he knows only what he has read or heard.

The narrator of *Iwein* is one of those with a sharply restricted point of view. In the episode of the three hundred maidens, he can only assume that the old couple in the park are man and wife and has only heard that the girl with them can read French. And, although he is sometimes aware of the hero's thoughts, at the end he has to confess that he has no certain knowledge of his future.[35] On one occasion the narrator must admit that he is also unable to interpret events properly, in the dialogue with Lady Love, who, after manipulating his responses to her questions, finally accuses him of being weak witted. This scene suggests that the author at times may be using him in the same way: as an unimaginative, naive straight man whose inappropriate comments emphasize the humor or irony of certain situations. When Laudine considers marrying Iwein, the narrator defends not only her, but all ladies, from the charge of fickleness. This digression serves Hartmann in three ways: it offers a bit of polite flattery to the female listeners, it reveals a remarkable obtuseness which emphasizes Laudine's fault, and it pleases the male audience by making them feel wiser than the narrator. The latter's credibility is also undermined by his claim that Keii was a great warrior (made just before he is easily unhorsed by Iwein), the assertion that his hero did not want to shame the steward (in spite of the heavy sarcasm directed at his fallen comrade), and other statements which are contradicted by the facts. It is clear that Hartmann intended that the story be interpreted on the basis of the events themselves and the statements of the characters, not on the basis of the words or, in certain instances, the silence of the narrator.[36]

Although the narrator cannot be trusted to render faithfully the reactions of the author to the separate incidents, he nevertheless performs many important functions. One is simply to break periodically the illusion of reality and limit the audience's involvement in the action. In this respect, *Iwein*, like some other medieval narratives, resembles Brecht's epic theater. Hartmann had things to say—not only the central message announced at the beginning, but also many lesser bits of wisdom—and he did not intend to waste them on listeners who were too intently following the hero's exploits. A comparison of his introduction with the opening lines of *Yvain* shows that from the very beginning Hartmann's purpose was quite different from Chrétien's. With a few perfunctory remarks about love, the Frenchman leaps at once into his story, which, told largely in the present tense, produces a strong feeling of dramatic immediacy. The German narrator, on the other hand, stresses that King Arthur lived in a previous age, maintains that he would rather live in his own times, and proceeds to tell his tale in the past tense.

Two examples of the narrator's intervention to alienate the audience from the action are seen in Iwein's battles with Askalon and with Gawein. In the former case, the narrator interrupts his description of the long conflict and refuses to give further details under the humorous pretext, developed at some length, that it is useless to do so since there were no other spectators to verify his words. The digression serves, of course, to extend the battle without a possibly boring repetition of blow on blow, but it also reminds the audience that they are listening to fiction—which, unlike life, must have a moral—and gives them an opportunity to reflect on the fact that Askalon is defending his property and the hero is the aggressor. In his account of the combat with Gawein, the narrator declines to present a complete description because everyone already knows so much about the bravery and skill of both warriors. After delaying the beginning of the battle with a lengthy expression of regret that the friends should fight each other, he twice interrupts it: first with a long explanation of how love and hate could coexist in one heart and later with an extended simile which compares the struggle to a financial transaction. The overall impression made by the scene

is that the didactic reflections are not so much a casual by-prod-
uct of the description of violence as ends in themselves. Such a
treatment is an expression of Hartmann's conviction, frequently evident in *Gregorius* and *Der arme Heinrich*, that ideas
are more important than deeds.

   To compensate for putting distance between his listeners and
the events described, the narrator attempts to establish a close
rapport between the listeners and himself by frequent references to himself, by addressing them directly, and by asso-
ciating himself with them through the use of *we* and *us*. His
success is apparent when a member of his fictional audience interrupts to question one of his statements. The goal to be
achieved through this intimate relationship seems to be the
gaining of support for the narrator's thoughts as expressed in
his digressions.

   Although evoked by events of the age of King Arthur, many of
the digressions have little to do with those times, but are instead
directed at Hartmann's contemporaries. They fall roughly into
two groups, the serious and the amusing, both of which appear to
have a more or less didactic purpose. A considerable amount of
irony is included, and it is occasionally difficult to know
whether or not a statement is to be taken at face value, which is
to say that the narrator, whose limitations are sometimes apparent when he comments on the actions, is not always reliable
when he generalizes from them. There are, however, a large
number of interpolations whose content is clear and relevant and
which seem to come directly from the author. These are not
arranged in any particular order that directly supports the
theme, but instead provide a broad and varied background of
practical maxims and aphorisms, which is especially appropriate
for a story of a man's progress from arrogance to true kindness.[37]

   The ironically amusing remarks of the narrator not only
lighten the general mood of what might otherwise have been a
rather somber tale, but also give occasional hints for its interpretation. His comment that he thought Laudine's court did
right to advise her to marry Iwein "because, if they all had
thought it a mistake, she would have taken him anyway," is a
droll reflection on the relations between advisers and monarchs

and, in addition, makes one wonder if Laudine really is motivated primarily by the welfare of her people. The suspicion is
increased when the narrator again interrupts her consultation
with the court to state: "Why say more—everything was as it
should be. There were many priests at hand and they performed
the ceremony at once." The humor of everything being as it
should be when a widow so hastily marries the slayer of her
husband can hardly be missed. However, to make sure that the
listeners catch the irony, he dismisses the matter with the blithe
report: "The dead man was forgotten as the living took over honors and land: all became his. A greater celebration was never
held in that country before or since." These and similar brief intrusions of the narrator demonstrate that Hartmann, like Wolfram, could smile at the errors of his sympathetic characters.

The longer digressions of the narrator reveal more about his
humor than the shorter ones. The argument between the
narrator and a personified Lady Love, who suddenly appears as
Iwein is leaving his bride for a year of tournaments, is both
amusing and ironic. The incongruity of an abstraction from the
minnesong assuming a speaking role in a verse epic adds an
element of broad comedy. This grows with her aggressive criticism of the narrator's version of the story, her rude demand that
he keep still, and her attempts to defend on a logical basis a
common, but far-fetched, conceit of a love song tradition which
even Hartmann's lyric verse had rejected.[38] However, there is
more here than slapstick and the ridiculing of a literary convention, for it is just this implausible figure who, according to the
narrator, was the irresistible force responsible for the unseemly
marriage of hero and heroine. It is also she who insists that King
Arthur did not actually contribute to the separation of Iwein
and Laudine. But her casuistry only serves to point out to the
audience that the supposedly all-wise King Arthur must indeed
share with Gawein the responsibility for the hero's downfall. A
dual purpose can also be seen in another lengthy digression—the extended simile of borrowing and lending, with its
comic (and untranslatable) play on words, that interrupts the
account of the battle with Gawein. It has a cheerful wit that,
against the background of the life-and-death struggle, could ap-

pear grotesque if its tone did not remind one that all this was, after all, not real life, but fiction. As for irony, we may well suspect that Hartmann is poking fun at an irrational means of arriving at truth and justice, just as Gottfried does after Isold's trial by ordeal.

As might be expected, the humor of *Iwein* is not limited to the intrusions of the narrator, but is a characteristic element of the author's style. The tone of the work, especially the first half, is set by Kalogrenant's account, which reveals him as a faint-hearted hero: afraid of the fierce beasts of the forest, more frightened by the monstrous shepherd, terrified by the violent storm, and eager to talk himself out of the joust with Askalon. The description of his inauspicious departure from the fountain caps a series of similar pictures that mark the tale as a ludicrous parody of knight-errantry. In addition to the figure of the timid knight, Kalogrenant's story contains a type of character which the Middle Ages found very amusing, the fantastically ugly human, here represented by the shepherd. It is easy to imagine the enjoyment of the listeners as his outlandish features were presented one by one in imaginatively grotesque detail and their laughter when he responds to the question of what kind of creature he is with the answer: "A man, as you can see." Wolfram, Wirnt von Grafenberg, and Heinrich von dem Türlin exploit the comic potential of similar beings. The laughter of Hartmann's audience, however, would soon have turned into a knowing smile with the ironic revelation that the monster is more sensible than the knight.

Keii, too, is an intrinsically humorous figure, representing the ubiquitous type of the confirmed braggart. During the journey to the spring, he ridicules the absent Iwein at length for boasting and praises himself extravagantly for his valor, his generous nature, and his modesty—all of which leads up to his ignominious defeat. The routine is repeated with considerable embellishment later on, when the queen is abducted. Keii's loud threats and declarations of great superiority over Meljakanz end with him hanging neatly from a tree, an object of sport to his comrades as they ride by toward their own comical discomfiture. The entire episode, while vividly illustrating the pride which goes before a fall, is thoroughly amusing.

Keii certainly has no sense of humor, and Kalogrenant may not have, but Lunete is knowingly mischievous and, like her creator, has a keen eye for laughable situations. Just before his first meeting with Laudine, Lunete teases Iwein by pretending that her mistress is very angry and, after bringing the two together, makes fun of his silence and apparent shyness. "You could sit a little closer," she scolds. "I'll promise that my lady won't bite you." Moreover, her subsequent troubles do not seem to diminish greatly the roguishness of her nature, as is seen when she prepares to trick Laudine into a compromising agreement. "Lady," she says in an ironic reference to her narrow escape from death, "I must phrase the oath so carefully that no one can accuse me of treachery."

The humor of Lunete is that of the clever, sharp-tongued underling who manipulates a superior. But most of the comedy of *Iwein* comes from incongruities: the timorous knight, the monstrous man, the discrepancy between Keii's words and his deeds. To these may be added Gawein's harried, unkempt, and countrified lord of the manor (perhaps a sly dig at one of Hartmann's contemporaries); a hermit, hiding fearfully from a naked madman who seems to him like a giant; a young lady who compulsively smears ointment all over the nude hero, even though specifically ordered to use only a little on his head; and, above all, a spring that terrorizes a country. The last disturbance of its water has no moral implications, and the vivid description of the raging storm and the exasperated, terrified citizens who curse the first man who settled there is highly amusing.

The use of sharp contrasts—between one person and another, appearance and true nature, expectation and fulfillment—which produces much of Hartmann's humor is also characteristic of other elements of his style. Keii sleeps while Gawein prepares his weapons and armor; the courtly Kalogrenant explains the knightly quest to the crude and ugly shepherd; the paradise at the spring is struck by a frightful tempest; Iwein, at the height of his glory, is threatened by the specter of the unchivalrous landowner; at the castle of the three hundred maidens, the hero and his host's daughter speak of the summer's beauty while the old couple talk of the coming winter; love and hate fill the hearts of Gawein and Iwein as they fight; two sisters represent the best and the worst of human nature.[39] Such juxta-positions of discordant factors facilitate the irony that permeates the work and is the most distinguishing feature of its style. It is an irony which, in many ways, constantly suggests to the listener that the adventures of which he hears may be important chiefly as parables.

Another stylistic device that Hartmann uses to emphasize ideas is doubling, certain aspects of which were discussed in the examination of *Iwein's* structure. The work contains numerous instances of actions being repeated, with differences that evoke comparisons. On Lunete's first visit to Arthur's court, she is greeted only by Iwein, but when she goes there a second time, she brings a greeting to everyone except him. We learn the story of Iwein's sojourn at Laudine's castle first from the narrator and the conversations of Laudine, Lunete, and the hero himself; later it is summarized, from a different point of view, by Lunete as she is awaiting execution for her involvement in the affair. A similar recapitulation occurs when the messenger follows Iwein's trail and hears of his rescue of Gawein's relatives and Lunete. When the hero first comes to the spring, he is trapped between the portcullises and is saved by Lunete, but on his return, she is the prisoner and must be freed by him. Then Iwein is confined again, and looks through a window to see three hundred sad women, which reminds the reader that he had looked through a window when a prisoner of Laudine and watched her grieving for Askalon. Lunete gives the hero a ring that saves his life; Laudine gives him one that is a symbol of her love. On two occasions Laudine is persuaded to make a promise without knowing its full implications, is talked into accepting Iwein as her husband, and sends a messenger to bring him into her country when he is already in her castle. Their marriage is twice discussed by the narrator, right after the wedding and once more at the end of the story. Iwein fights against two Arthurian knights, the basest and the noblest. One black, wild man of the wilderness frightens a knight, another frightens a hermit. In each instance, the similarities and differences between the first and second occurence throw light on the development of the plot while adding depth to its meaning.

Although the separate incidents in *Iwein* often evoke a proverb from the narrator, he does not explain them in terms of his theme, preferring to have the listeners do this for themselves on the basis of the character's own words. He frequently interprets this direct discourse to some extent with brief comments which immediately precede or follow it, such as: "Sir Keii was happy because he had found an object for his jeers [and] . . . said"; "The lady was happy at this good news [and] . . . said"; "The knight with the lion felt very sorry for him and said"; "When no one appeared, he was concerned and said"; and "Touched by their misfortune, the knight sighed deeply and said." For the most part, however, the story moves forward in monologues and conversations, with much less manifest guidance by the narrator than is found in the works of Hartmann's contemporaries or in his own earlier compositions.[40] There is also little attempt to adorn the plot with the detailed descriptions of fine clothing, beautiful women, splendid festivals, and fierce battles which are characteristic of other Arthurian novels, including Hartmann's source and his own *Erec*.

Iwein was composed in the prevailing narrative verse form of its times: the tetrameter rhymed couplet that is frequently shortened to trimeter and usually has masculine, but occasionally feminine, rhyme. The versification of the work is perhaps the most skillful in Middle High German epic literature. There are few obvious verse and rhyme fillers, and the sentence structure closely approximates that of normal speech. The language emphasies clarity and simplicity of expression, has a minimum of trite, specifically literary phrases, and employs relatively few adjectives and similes. It is markedly courtly, avoiding epithets and the characteristically heroic vocabulary. This largely unadorned style is occasionally embellished by a humorous playing with words and by the use of metaphors. When the narrator comments on the gatekeeper at the castle of the three hundred women, he exploits the word *schalk* (knave), just as he does *süeze* (kind) in praising the younger Countess of Black Thorn and *gelten* (to repay) when he describes the battle between Iwein and Gawein. Most of the metaphors are short and of a religious nature, but one, that dealing with love and hate in the same vessel, is extended to almost sixty verses.[41]

To compensate for the simple, almost austere style, Hartmann presents certain figures and incidents in a way that creates overtones of meaning and relationship which stimulate the imagination and curiosity of the listener. The first of these suggestive phenomena is the fantastic shepherd. Although he serves an obvious function in the development of the plot and can also be justified as providing a comic interlude, the medieval audience, brought up on *exempla* and parables, would have wondered if there weren't more to him than this. Their suspicions would have been confirmed later, when they noticed the similarity between the shepherd and the mad hero and recognized the former as a prefiguration of Iwein.[42] With regard to the significance of this relationship, the author was apparently satisfied to have each listener find his own answer. The second figure to exhibit symbolic qualities is the clear, cold spring with its lovely linden, melodious bird song, precious metals and jewels, and violent, stormy nature when disturbed. The connection between it and its mistress is established as soon as Laudine appears—stunningly beautiful as she tears her hair and clothing in a frenzy of grief and rage—and is confirmed when we learn that her security and honor depend on the defense of the spring. One can gain esthetic pleasure from the relationship without knowing whether its primary purpose is for the spring to interpret Laudine's character or for the lady, as an embodiment of its elemental forces, to add meaning to the spring.[43]

Iwein's strange life in the wilderness is as unusual as the herdsman and the spring, and as provocative. With regard to structure, it supplies a clear-cut division between the hero's earlier and later adventures; and from the religious standpoint, it provides an adequate and appropriate penalty for his *superbia* (the medieval audience would have thought of the mad King Nebuchadnezzar, living with the beasts of the field and eating grass in punishment for similar arrogance). However, since Hartmann made this episode half again as long as its source, one can again expect something more, which is found in the association between the madman and the hermit. Kalogrenant's definition of the knightly quest and Iwein's unrestrained pursuit of honor portray a society whose members are in ruthless competition with each other. Hero and hermit, on the other hand, establish a primitive community of mutual aid. To be sure, it is based on necessity rather than love, but it is successful and it prepares the listener for the better, though still simple, society of both help and devotion: that made up of Iwein and the lion. The picture of the cooperation in the wilderness lends to the hero's future development social connotations, which are reinforced by the circumstances of his healing, for the description of the girl rubbing ointment on him may be symbolic as well as humorous. There is an obvious parallel to the parable of the good neighbor, the Samaritan; three people encounter an injured, naked man; one goes to help him, rubs (or pours) a medicinal material over him, supplies him with a horse, and takes him to a place where he is cared for. A medieval audience would have noticed the similarity between the stories at once and understood its relevance.[44]

The most important emblematic function in the novel is served by the lion. The fact that Hartmann is careful to remove all the slapstick connected with this figure in *Yvain* implies that he intended it to play a more serious role than that assigned by Chrétien, even though he does not expand its direct participation in the action. To its character as a lion, Hartmann adds a moral concept, the nature of which can be guessed by examining his references to it. It is called "the noble beast" when involved in a life-and-death struggle with a fire-breathing, foul-smelling dragon (certainly a symbol of evil). The lion joins the hero just after he performs his first purely unselfish deed, brings him food by day, and watches over him at night. In an unparalleled example of prescience, the narrator states that they remained together until death. During the scene at the spring, the lion exhibits the ultimate in devotion, showing Iwein what true loyalty is, and in the battles that follow it repeatedly risks its life to save his. The Arthurian court flees from it. All this points to the idea of *rehtiu güete*. When Iwein, on his pilgrimage of expiation, identifies himself as "The Knight with the Lion," he presumably wishes to be known as the man of true kindness.[45]

A final example of Hartmann's addition of symbolic overtones is seen in the combat with Gawein. It is not a personal affair—the two knights are agents, not principals—but a conflict between social theories. Gawein represents individual aggrandizement and a closed society of manners and customs, Iwein the idea of altruistic service and the community of mankind. Neither is victorious, and the hero and his lion go to another land where both they and that which they represent can be accepted.[46]

Notes

1. The introductions to Hartmann's *Der arme Heinrich* and *Iwein* describe the author as a knight, educated, and a vassal at Aue. One of his crusade songs tells of his preparation to take the cross, but scholars are divided about whether he went on the crusade of 1189–90 or that of 1197–98. The approximate date of decease is indicated when Gottfried von Strassburg, in verses 4621–55 of his *Tristan und Isold* (ca. 1210), praises Hartmann as a living poet and Heinrich von dem Türlin, in verse 2348 of *Die Krone* (ca. 1220), mourns his death. With regard to the period of his writing, there is a difference of opinion about whether he began around 1180 or some ten years later. However, it is clear that *Iwein*, which is generally accepted as his last work, was completed before 1204, since Wolfram von Eschenbach mentioned an episode from it at about that time (*Parzival*, paragraph 253, verse 10). As to his native region, scholars agree that Hartmann's speech was Alemannic, and some believe it was specifically that of the area north and northwest of Zurich. Henricus Sparnaay, *Hartmann von Aue: Studien zu einer Biographie*, 2 vols. (Tübingen: Niemeyer, 1933), 1:14–17, presents linguistic evidence to support this conclusion, which receives confirmation from the fact that illustrations in the Weingarten and Manesse song manuscripts show Hartmann wearing the armorial bearings of the Wesperbühl family, which had property in the area in question. Further possibilities are discussed by Peter Wapnewsky, *Hartmann von Aue*, Sammlung Metzler, no. 17 (Stuttgart: Metzler, 1962), pp. 4–9; Bertha Schwarz, "Hartmann von Aue," *Die deutsche Literatur des Mittlalters: Verfasserlexikon*, 5 vols. (Berlin: Walter de Gruyter, 1933–55), 2:203; Friedrich Neumann, "Hartmann von Aue," *Verfasserlexikon*, 5:322–23; and others.

Since the hero of Hartmann's *Gregorius* attended a monastic school on an island, it has frequently been suggested that the account of his education may have been drawn from the author's own experience. Young Gregorius's schooling began at six, and he had fully mastered Latin by the time he was ten. He completed the study of theology in the following three years and had finished one year of law when, at fourteen, his formal education was unexpectedly terminated. Aloys Schulte, "Die Reichenau und der Adel: Tatsachen und Wirkungen,"

Die Kultur der Abtei Reichenau, 2 vols. (Munich: Münchner Drucke, 1925), 1:580, does not find any Hartmann in the records of Reichenau, but that does not mean that the poet could not have been a student there.

2. It has been argued that the first one thousand verses of *Iwein* use older forms than does *Der arme Heinrich* and that the novella, therefore, must have been written during an interruption in the composition of the novel. Most scholars, however, do not accept this conclusion.

3. The *Vie du pape Grégoire* is by an unknown poet of the twelfth century. It has not been possible to establish a plausible connection between the hero of the work and any of the seven popes of this name who lived prior to its composition.

4. Pentti Tilvis, "Über die unmittelbaren Vorlagen von Hartmanns *Erec* and *Iwein,* Ulrichs *Lanzelet* und Wolframs *Parzival,*" *Neuphilologische Mitteilungen* 60 (1959): 29, states that either Hartmann had other French sources for his *Erec* and *Iwein* in addition to Chrétien's romances or he used versions of these which were different from the ones extant. There is an extensive literature on the question of Chrétien's sources. A. C. L. Brown, "The Knight of the Lion," *PMLA* 20 (1905): 705, concludes that he used a single Welsh tale. In "Iwain: A Study in the Origins of Arthurian Romance," *Studies and Notes in Philology and Literature* 8 (1903): 1–147, the same author gives an extensive account of possible Welsh source material.

5. The Icelandic versions of Chrétien's *Erec* and *Yvain* have recently been translated into English by Foster W. Blaisdell, Jr., and Marianne E. Kalinke, in *Erex Saga and Ívens Saga* (Lincoln and London: University of Nebraska Press, 1977). In their introduction, p. xviii, the translators agree with previous scholars that the Swedish translator used the Old Norse as well as the French work.

6. Hendricus Sparnaay, "Zu Iwein Owein," *Zeitschrift für romanische Philologie* 46 (1926): 519–20, states that *Iban* was based on Hartmann's version and at least one other source. Rudolf Zenker, *Forschungen zur Artusepik: I, Ivainstudien* (Halle: Niemeyer, 1921), pp. 209–12, discusses the scholarship on this matter.

7. Emil Henrici, ed., *Iwein: Der Ritter mit dem Löwen* (Halle: Waisenhaus, 1891), p. xii.

8. The Gace Brulé song is "Ire d'amors ke en mon cuer repaire," while that of Hartmann is "Ich muoz von rehte den tac iemer minnen." The German song would also have used the melody, which is extant, of its French model.

9. Henrici, *Iwein,* p. viii.

10. An account of the extensive literature on Wirnt's debt to Hart-

mann appears in J. W. Thomas, *Wigalois: The Knight of Fortune's Wheel* (Lincoln and London: University of Nebraska Press, 1977), pp. 81–83.

11. Friedrich Ranke, ed., *Gottfried von Strassburg, Tristan und Isold*, 14th ed. (Zurich: Weidmann, 1969), lines 4621–37.

12. Friedrich Neumann, *Kleinere Schriften zur deutschen Philologie des Mittelalters* (Berlin: Walter de Gruyter, 1969), p. 50; Hans Naumann and Hans Steinger, eds., *Hartmann von Aue, Erec / Iwein* (Leipzig: Philipp Reclam, 1933), p. 23. Extensive discussions of Hartmann's literary influence appear in Sparnaay, *Hartmann von Aue*, 2:102–6 and Henrici, *Iwein*, pp. vi–xii.

13. Johannes Erben, "Zu Hartmanns *Iwein*," *Zeitschrift für deutsche Philologie* 87 (1968): 344, and Hans Szklenar, "Iwein-Fresken auf Schloss Rodeneck in Südtirol," *Bulletin Bibliographique de la Société Internationale Arthurienne* 27 (1975): 172–80.

14. In recent years points of view which are close to the traditional one have been reflected in studies by Hildegard Emmel, Bert Nagel, Ernst von Reusner, Kurt Ruh, and Theodorus van Stockum, among others, while the importance of various aspects of the Christian ethic (as opposed to Arthurian manners) for the work has been stressed by Michael Batts, Thomas Cramer, Rolf Endres, Johannes Erben, Anna Matthias, Arnim Meng, Humphrey Milnes, Walter Ohly, Hugh Sacker, Günther Schweikle, Herbert Wiegand, and others. Other Hartmann scholars either represent a middle position or have not emphasized the ideological basis of *Iwein*.

15. Critics are divided about the specific meanings of *rehtiu güete, saelde,* and *êre* as they appear in this verse, especially the meanings of the first two, and each has his favorite translation. The matter is discussed most fully by Thomas Cramer, "*Saelde* und *êre* in Hartmanns *Iwein*," *Euphorion* 60 (1966): 30–47; Bert Nagel, "Hartmann zitiert Reinmar: *Iwein* 1–30 und *MF* 150/10–18," *Euphorion* 63 (1969): 6–40; and Rolf Endres, "Der Prolog von Hartmanns *Iwein*," and "Die Bedeutung von *güete* und die Dieseitigkeit der Artusromane Hartmanns," *Deutsche Vierteljahresschrift für Literaturwissenschaft und Geistesgeschichte* 40 (1966): 509–37, and 44 (1970): 595–612. The translation given above is close to that proposed by Endres and (with respect to *saelde* and *êre*) by Cramer.

16. Since the definition does not appear in *Yvain*, one must assume that Hartmann attached considerable significance to it. Thomas Cramer, *Hartmann von Aue: Iwein* (Berlin: De Gruyter, 1968), p. 181, believes that Kalogrenant is not expressing his true opinion of the knightly quest, but is only trying to explain it in words that the herdsman can understand. However, Walter Ohly, *Die heils-*

geschichtliche Struktur der Epen Hartmanns von Aue (Berlin: Reuter, 1958), p. 102; Michael Batts, "Hartmanns' Humanitas: A New Look at *Iwein*," *Germanic Studies in Honor of Edward Henry Sehrt* (Coral Gables: University of Miami Press, 1968), p. 40; and others, are doubtless correct in assuming that Kalogrenant meant just what he said. J. M. Clifton-Everest, "Christian Allegory in Hartmann's *Iwein*," *Germanic Review* 48 (1973): 257, thinks that Kalogrenant's definition expressed the knight's own ideas correctly, but that these were not held by the Arthurian community in general. Still, the subsequent words and deeds of the other members of the court demonstrate that they shared his view of *aventiure*.

17. The traditional *Iwein* scholarship assumes that Hartmann saw nothing reprehensible in his hero's actions during this adventure. There are clear indications that this view is incorrect. Cramer, *Hartmann*, pp. 185–86, cites documents which show that an attack on property without due warning was illegal in the early thirteenth century. Moreover, Hartmann's account is significantly different from that in *Yvain*: he twice repeats Chrétien's statement that Askalon was mortally wounded, he calls Iwein's pursuit unmannerly (*âne zuht*), and he has him strike his opponent as he flees. The three most recent attempts to prove that Hartmann did not condemn his hero are no more convincing than their predecessors. They are: Harald Scholler, "Wâ sint diu werc? die rede hoere ich wol: Ein Beitrag zur Interpretation von Hartmanns *Iwein*," *Husbanding the Golden Grain: Studies in Honor of Henry W. Nordmeyer* (Ann Arbor: University of Michigan Press, 1973), p. 300; Paul Salmon, "Ane zuht: Hartmann von Aue's Criticism of Iwein," *Modern Language Review* 69 (1974): 556–61; and Robert E. Lewis, *Symbolism in Hartmann's Iwein*, Göppinger Arbeiten zur Germanistik, no. 154 (Göppingen: Kümmerle, 1975), p. 100.

18. Iwein's ridicule of Keii compares unfavorably with Askalon's treatment of Kalogrenant and Yvain's behavior toward Kes. The narrator's comment that Iwein did not want to shame Keii is ironic. Theodorus van Stockum, "Hartmann von Aues *Iwein*. Sein Problem und seine Probleme," *Mededelingen der koninklijke Nederlandse Akademie van Wetenschappen, Afd. Letterkunde* 26 (1963): 115, wishes to render Hartmann's *schimpflichen* (mockingly), used to describe Iwein's words to his fallen opponent, with the Modern German *scherzhaft-ironisch* (jokingly ironic) in order to show that Hartmann is not condemning his hero. His translation, though possible, is not at all probable in this situation.

19. The critical attitude of most contemporary scholarship toward Iwein is first seen in the works of Sparnaay. In *Hartmann von Aue,*

2:49, he writes: "Der Dichter nennt Iwein also zuchtlos, tadelt sein schimpfliches Betragen dem besiegten Feind gegenüber und betont, dass seine Liebe zunächst nur sinnliches Begehren sei. Dann kann man doch wirklich nicht behaupten . . . dass Iwein bei H. von vornherein als das Idealbild des höfischen Ritters erscheine."

20. This incident, which Lunete recounts, gives the first indication that the hero is potentially superior to the other Arthurian knights even though he at first shares their values. It also serves the plot by initiating a chain of interactions between Lunete and Iwein which stretches from beginning to end and facilitates the development of the story.

21. The most detailed study of the monologue is by Max Wehrli, "Iweins Erwachen," *Formen mittelalterlicher Erzählung* (Zurich: Atlantis, 1969), pp. 177–93.

22. Although neither Hartmann nor Chrétien gives a reason for Aliers's attack, one may assume that the count wants to marry the lady (probably to get her land) because of the close similarity of this episode to one in *Gregorius* and because there are certain parallels to the Harpin incident. The motif also appears in Wolfram's *Parzival*.

23. The earlier scholarship took the narrator seriously and considered Hartmann's generous treatment of Laudine an improvement over Chrétien's cynicism. Some recent critics have also taken him seriously but have considered the attempt to make Laudine a sympathetic character, in view of her actions, a blunder on the part of the author. Endres, "Der Prolog," p. 516, is more perceptive when he calls the narrator's defense an "unorganische Zutat" which expresses Hartmann's ideas about women in general and was not really intended to apply to the immediate situation, but he, too, misses the irony. Erben, "Hartmanns *Iwein*," p. 349, ignores the narrator's comments and states that Laudine's decision to marry the hero was based on inordinate ambition. The same opinion is held by Anna Susanna Matthias, "Der Entwicklungsgedanke in Hartmanns Artusromanen" (Dr. Phil. dissertation, University of Hamburg, 1951), p. 41. Her study contains, pp. 41–43, the fullest treatment of the development of Laudine. Michael S. Batts, "Das Ritterideal in Hartmanns *Iwein*," *Doitsu Bungaku* 37 (1966): 90, sees no development here nor any indication that Hartmann was really interested in the Laudine figure.

24. Ohly, *Heilsgeschichtliche Struktur*, p. 108, sees in the emphasis on the heroine's impatience sufficient evidence that the attempt to defend her against a charge of inconstancy was ironic. He thinks that Laudine was attracted primarily by Iwein's social position. The recent attempt by Theodor Priesack to excuse Laudine is not convincing: "Laudines Dilemma," in *Sagen mit Sinne: Festschrift für Marie-*

Luise Dittrich, Göppinger Arbeiten zur Germanistik, no. 180 (Göppingen: Kümmerle, 1976), pp. 109–32.

25. The scene between Laudine and her subjects, as Chrétien describes it, has been significantly altered by Hartmann. In the French story they urge her to remarry, and she—with pretended reluctance—accedes; in the German account Laudine has the seneschal first announce her decision to marry Iwein and then ask for their concurrence. The change not only gives the heroine a more headstrong character, but also makes it clearer that she is not primarily interested in the welfare of her people. The passage in which the subjects express their approval is a quotation from the scene in *Der arme Heinrich* in which the hero's family advises him to wed the farmer's daughter. Hartmann, with evident irony, thus invites his audience to compare the appropriateness of the two marriages.

26. Xenja von Ertzdorff, "Spiel der Interpretation: Der Erzähler in Hartmanns *Iwein*," *Festgabe für Friedrich Maurer* (Düsseldorf: Schwann, 1968), pp. 141–45, points out that in Chrétien's version Laudine speaks of love twice here, repeatedly in the message she sends when the hero has overstayed his leave, and again at the end, when he is seeking a reconciliation. In Hartmann's work, on the other hand, Laudine's *êre*, not love, is stressed on the first two of these occasions. It is also noteworthy that Chrétien says nothing about Laudine's becoming more fond of her husband because of the honor which she is shown by Arthur's visit. The German version wishes to demonstrate that Laudine exhibits the same *superbia* as Iwein.

27. Jan C. W. C. De Jong, *Hartmann von Aue als Moralist in seinen Artusepen* (Amsterdam: van Soest, 1964), p. 95, writes: "Dass Laudine Iwein bei der ersten Begegnung nach seiner Abenteuerfahrt nicht wieder erkennt, muss symbolisch gedeutet werden: zwar ist Iwein auf dem besten Weg zur Rehabilitierung, jedoch er ist noch nicht würdig, von Laudine als Gatte begrüsst zu werden." Ohly, *Heilsgeschichtliche Struktur*, p. 118, comments: "Den Iwein, der ihr namenlos und ohne gesellschaftliche Anerkennung gegenübertritt, erkennt sie deshalb nicht, weil sie sein tieferes Selbst nicht kennt . . . weil ihr nicht der alte höfische Iwein gegenübersteht, sondern der gewandelte, leidtragende Namenlose, deshalb ist sie blind." Erben, "Hartmanns *Iwein*, p. 355, sees the beginning of Laudine's redemption in the words of her farewell. Endres, "Der Prolog," p. 532, says, "Er verbirgt seinen Namen und seine Identität nicht aus dem Gefühl seiner Nichtigkeit vor Gott, sondern aus dem Gefühl seiner Nichtigkeit und Schuldbeladenheit vor Laudine."

28. Arthur Witte, "Hartmann von Aue und Kristian von Troyes," *Beiträge zur Geschichte der deutschen Sprache und Literatur* 53

(1929): 161, and Kurt Ruh, "Zur Interpretation von Hartmanns *Iwein*," *Hartmann von Aue*, Wege der Forschung, no. 359 (Darmstadt: Wissenschaftliche Buchgesellschaft, 1973), p. 422, think Laudine's remorse and supplication inconsistent with her character and a blunder on the part of the author. Ernst von Reusner, "Iwein," *Deutsche Vierteljahresschrift für Literaturwissenschaft und Geistesgeschichte* 46 (1972): 503n, considers the heroine only a symbol of courtly love and therefore not subject to moral evaluation. On the other hand, Matthias, "Der Entwicklungsgedanke," pp. 42, 76; Ohly, *Heilsgeschichtliche Struktur*, p. 124; and De Jong, *Hartmann*, p. 96, find Laudine's reactions a natural result of her moral development.

29. A comparison of Hartmann's treatment of Lunete with that of his source is enlightening with regard to her character development. In the French version she is not the messenger who is sent to denounce the hero and therefore has no opportunity to express her personal resentment at his failure. She does not admit that her own anger was to blame for her imprisonment or that she considered her own advantage in helping the hero. Hartmann emphasizes her atonement for *superbia* by having her on her knees and commending her soul to God when Iwein arrives to save her, whereas Chrétien only mentions that she had already made confession. Eva-Maria Carne, *Die Frauengestalten bei Hartmann von Aue: Ihre Bedeutung im Aufbau und Gehalt der Epen* (Marburg: Elwert, 1970), p. 38, considers Lunete the chief representative of true kindness from beginning to end, but Wolfram is certainly more perceptive when he twice condemns her early action in advising Laudine to marry the slayer of her husband.

30. Whether or not Hartmann intended to present the Arthurian court and its ethic as ideals is a basic and controversial problem. During the nineteenth and the first third of the twentieth century, critics assumed that he did. Then Ernst Scheunemann, *Artushof und Abenteuer: Zeichnung höfischen Daseins in Hartmanns Erec*, Deutschkundliche Arbeiten, ser. A, no. 8 (Breslau: Maruschke, 1937), p. 116, challenged this assumption when he wrote: "Trotz der Betonung des Artusbereiches in 2657 ff. ist die Rolle, die Artus im *Iwein* spielt, eine andere als im *Erec*. Der Artusbereich ist in seiner fraglosen Gültigkeit erschüttert," and went on to point out the inability of the court to help outsiders or even to protect itself. However, he did not question the standards of the Arthurian society or try to explain why the author portrayed it as ineffectual. These matters were first treated by Matthias and Ohly in the fifties, and, soon afterward, Hugh Sacker, "An Interpretation of Hartmann's *Iwein*," *Germanic*

Review 36 (1961): 5, expressed a view which was reflected in much of the subsequent scholarship. "If one took as a criterion the *actions* of the various members of the Round Table," he wrote, "(and not the statements about them), one might well conclude that this company consisted of a weak and passive king, a number of well-intentioned but quite useless knights—whose seneschal Keii is not even well-intentioned—and Gawein: a hero whose great abilities are perpetually misdirected. On closer inspection it would, I think, appear that what renders this company so ineffectual is its preoccupation with its own honor." Some of the later criticism interprets Hartmann's portrayal of the Arthurian society as being somewhat harsher. Günther Schweikle, "Zum *Iwein* Hartmanns von Aue: Strukturale Korrespondenzen und Oppositionen," *Probleme des Erzählens in der Weltliteratur: Festschrift für Käte Hamburger zum 75. Geburtstag* (Stuttgart: Klett, 1971), p. 17, says, "Der Artusritter vertritt ein Menschentum, das sich einem erstarrten elitären *êre*-Begriff unterordnet," and calls *Iwein* (p. 21) "eine Art Anti-Artusroman." Horst Pütz, "Artus-Kritik in Hartmanns *Iwein*," *Germanisch-romanische Monatsschrift* 22 (1972): 197, writes, "Mit *Iwein* überwindet auch Hartmann selbst die Artuswelt. Mit diesem Epos kehrt Hartmann daher nicht eigentlich zur arthurischen Epik zurück, sondern hier wendet er sich deutlich kritisch davon ab. Damit passt der *Iwein* recht gut im Anschluss an die Werke mit religiöser Thematik an das Ende seines Schaffens." Herbert Wiegand, *Studien zur Minne und Ehe in Wolframs Parzival und Hartmanns Artusepik*, Quellen und Forschungen zur Sprach- und Kulturgeschichte der Germanischen Völker, 49 (Berlin: De Gruyter, 1972), p. 285, speaks of the "Artusrittergesinnung, der jede sittliche Verankerung fehlt und die nur kriegerische Wertvorstellungen mit der *êre* als obersten Wert kennt." Carne, *Frauengestalten*, p. 130, refers to the ideals of Arthur's court as "leere Form." Marie Theres Nölle, *Formen der Darstellung in Hartmanns Iwein*, Europäische Hochschulschriften, ser. 1, no. 89 (Bern: Lang, 1974), p. 69, states, "Die erste Stufe, die Iwein zu bewältigen hat, ist die Emanzipation von den Masstäben, die ihm der Artushof gesetzt hat. Gerade die Werte, die er sich am Hof angeeignet hat, darunter vor allem die durch Tüchtigkeit im Kampf erworbene *êre* und das elitäre Selbstbewusstsein der auf sich selbst konzentrierten und geschlossenen Hofgesellschaft, lassen ihn scheitern." Gert Kaiser, *Textauslegung und gesellschaftliche Selbstdeutung: Aspekte einer sozialgeschichtlichen Interpretation von Hartmanns Artusepen* (Frankfurt: Athenäum, 1973), p. 112n, and Robert Lewis, *Symbolism*, p. 65, are more generous. The one mentions the "schon häufiger beobachtete

Tendenz, dass der Artushof im *Iwein* einiges von seiner Vorbildlichkeit eingebüsst hat"; the other calls the court "a generally well-intentioned but inevitably bumbling and mistake-ridden society."

31.   Ohly, *Heilgeschichtliche Struktur*, p. 96; Schweikle, "Zum *Iwein*," p. 17; and Hans-Werner Eroms, *"Vreude" bei Hartmann von Aue*, Medium Aevum: Philologische Studien, no. 20 (Munich: Fink, 1970), p. 135, attempt to reconcile the praise of Arthur in the opening lines with the story as a whole by pointing out that Hartmann stresses in his introduction that the king is a figure of the dead past, a literary character, as opposed to Iwein, who comes to represent the morality of the author's own day. Endres, "Der Prolog," pp. 533–34, considers Hartmann's praise to be no more than a standard rhetorical convention of his time, the purpose of which was to arouse the interest of the audience by exploiting a well-known name. His conclusion, p. 536, is "Das Exempel vom König Artus im Prolog ist ein Versatzstück, das isoliert vor der Erzählung steht."

32.   H. B. Willson, "The Role of Keii in Hartmann's *Iwein*," *Medium Aevum* 30 (1961): 146, sees the seneschal's literary function as that of a contrast figure. Eroms, *"Vreude,"* p. 141, disagrees, saying, "So ist Keii weniger Kontrastfigur zur höfischen Gesellschaft als verhärteter Pol dessen, was sie an konventionellen Zügen aufweist; mit ihm wird eine charakteristische Lebensweise des höfischen Menschen [*vreude*] ad absurdum geführt." Armin Meng, *Vom Sinn des ritterlichen Abenteuers bei Hartmann von Aue* (Zurich: Juris, 1967), p. 70, speaks in a similar vein about Gawein and Arthur: "Dass Gawein sich für einen ungerechtfertigten Erbanspruch einsetzt, mag auf den ersten Blick befremdlich erscheinen. Vermutlich wird hier, wie bei der Bitte des Meljakanz, wieder eine an sich gute Tradition ad absurdum geführt. Wie Artus jede Bitte erfüllen muss, selbst wenn sie die Ordnung am Hof gefährdet, so setzt sich Gawein eben für jede Hilfesuchenden ein, ungeachtet dessen, ob er damit auf der Seite des Rechts kämpft." Hartmann's method of discrediting the Arthurian community, accordingly, is to exaggerate their traditional characteristics ad absurdum.

33.   In comparing the piety of *Iwein* with that of Hartmann's other works, Sparnaay, *Hartmann von Aue*, 2:101, says, "Die Innigkeit seiner Gottesverbundenheit steigt vom Erec über Gregor und Armen Heinrich zum Iwein in ununterbrochener Linie empor." De Jong, *Hartmann*, pp. 90–95, lists and evaluates the references to God in *Iwein*.

34.   There have been thirteen other more or less detailed structural analyses of *Iwein* published in the past twenty-five years. The most recent of these, by Joachim Berger, "Der Aufbau von Hartmanns *Iwein*," *Amsterdamer Beiträge zur älteren Germanistik* 8

(1975): 33–57, and by Rolf Selbmann, "Strukturschema und Opera-
toren in Hartmanns *Iwein*," *Deutsche Vierteljahresschrift für Literaturwissenschaft und Geistesgeschichte* 50 (1976): 60–83, include
reviews of their predecessors.

35. Some medieval scribes were dissatisfied with this indefinite
conclusion and added endings of their own, one of which may have
been written during Hartmann's lifetime. An account of the false endings is contained in Christoph Gerhardt, "*Iwein*-Schlüsse," *Literatur-
wissenschaftliches Jahrbuch der Görres-Gesellschaft* 13 (1972): 13–39.

36. Criticism of the narrator is divided into that which identifies
him with the author and that which believes his opinions to be sometimes at variance with Hartmann's. The former view is held by
Hans-Peter Kramer, *Erzählerbemerkungen und Erzählerkommentare
in Chrestiens und Hauptmanns Erec und Iwein*, Göppinger Arbeiten
zur Germanistik, no. 35 (Göppingen: Kümmerle, 1971), p. 11, but
most of the recent scholarship considers the narrator to be a character
whom the author manipulates as he does the others. Ertzdorff, "Spiel
der Interpretation," p. 157, calls particular attention to the fact that
in important scenes the narrator discreetly withdraws and leaves
interpretation to the audience. William H. Jackson, "Some Obser-
vations on the Status of the Narrator in Hartmann von Aue's *Erec*
and *Iwein*," *Forum for Modern Language Studies* 6 (1970): 67, notes
that the narrator of *Iwein* "has become more questioning, less
self-confident in his telling" than the narrator of *Erec*.

37. The didactic passages are collected and discussed by van
Stockum, "Hartmann von Aues *Iwein*," pp. 32–36, and De Jong, *Hartmann*, pp. 100–106.

38. This appearance of a personified Lady Love in a narrative
work was probably the source of Ulrich von Liechtenstein's idea, in
his *Frauendienst*, of disguising himself as a figure whom he calls Lady
Venus, but who is in fact the Frau Minne of the minnesong.

39. Hartmann's use of contrasts is discussed chiefly in Siegfried
Grosse, "Die Wirkung des Kontrasts in den Dichtungen Hartmanns
von Aue," *Wirkendes Wort* 15 (1965): 29–39. Grosse examines particularly the contrasts between alternating scenes.

40. Herta Zutt, "Die Rede bei Hartmann von Aue," *Der Deutsch-
unterricht* 14 (1962): 78, writes, "Der gesamte Iweinroman ist ein
Spiel mit Worten und um Worte; sie sind die Mittel, mit denen die
Personen ihre Mitmenschen in die eine oder andere Richtung lenken,
je nach dem, wie ihnen der Sinn steht. Das gesprochene Wort wird
zum Angelpunkt der Handlung."

41. Norman J. Fry, "A Comparative Study of Metaphor in the
Ywain Legend" (Ph.D. dissertation, Stanford University, 1973), pp.
252–60, examines the two-hundred-odd metaphors which Hartmann

uses and notes especially his partiality for those having to do with religion.

42. Humphrey Milnes, "The Play of Opposites in *Iwein*," *German Life and Letters* 14 (1961), p. 253, calls the wild man "the representative of the primitive but vital level to which Iwein returned for his new start in life." Nölle, *Formen der Darstellung*, p. 36, suggests that the shepherd embodies an important and unavoidable station on the road of Iwein's self-development.

43. Sacker, "An Interpretation," p. 9, suggests a Freudian symbolism which associates the spring with Laudine and the tree with Askalon. D. G. Mowatt, "Tristan's Mothers and Iwein's Daughters," *German Life and Letters* 23 (1969): 29, connects the spring to Lunete and postulates an Oedipus relationship to the tree figure (first Askalon, then Iwein). Reusner, "Iwein," p. 502, identifies Laudine and the spring with courtly love. Robert Lewis, *Symbolism*, p. 69, calls the spring a symbol of Laudine and her defenselessness and adds, "Through the storms which occur when it is disturbed, the 'brunne' is symbolically linked with chaos and destruction, yet in its tranquility and in the beautiful music of the birds before and after the storm, the 'brunne' comes to symbolize beauty and delight."

44. Ohly, *Heilsgeschichtliche Struktur*, p. 7, connects the story of the good Samaritan to all of Hartmann's narrative works. Michael Batts, "Hartmann's Humanitas," p. 44, sees the anointing as a symbol of Iwein's rebirth. H. B. Willson, "Love and Charity in Hartmann's *Iwein*," *Modern Language Review* 57 (1962): 218; A. T. Hatto, "'Der Aventiure Meine' in Hartmann's *Iwein*," *Mediaeval German Studies: Presented to Frederick Norman* (London: University of London Institute of Germanic Studies, 1965), p. 97; Meng, *Ritterliches Abenteuer*, p. 60; Wehrli, "Iweins Erwachen," p. 186; and Robert Lewis, *Symbolism*, p. 33, call attention to the similarity to either the anointing of Jesus by Mary, the sister of Martha, or the Easter scene at the sepulcher when the three Marys come to anoint the body of Jesus, or both. They believe that Hartmann wished to imply by the analogy that the hero was being consecrated to new, Christian goals. Clifton-Everest, "Christian Allegory," p. 253, considers the anointing to be a type of Christian baptism. A. Wolf, "Erzählkunst und verborgener Schriftsinn: Zur Diskussion um Chrétiens *Yvain* und Hartmanns *Iwein*," *Sprachkunst* 2 (1971): 36, sees nothing more in the episode than humor.

45. Most recent scholars have regarded the lion as being to some extent a symbol and have suggested a number of different interpretations of its symbolism, including faithfulness, nobility, the ennobled natural forces of man, justice, and Christ. Others point to its

ideological function, as opposed to symbolism, and note that it gives an example of true knightly virtues and serves as an agent of God.

46. The translation which follows was made from the text as it appears in G. F. Benecke, K. Lachmann, and Ludwig Wolff, *Iwein: Eine Erzählung von Hartmann von Aue*, 2 vols., 7th ed. (Berlin: Walther De Gruyter, 1968).

Iwein

The Knight with the Lion

He who turns his heart to true kindness will have God's favor and man's esteem. One sees this with the noble King Arthur, who knew how to strive for fame with a knightly spirit. He lived in such a manner that he wore the crown of honor in his time, and his name does even now. That is why his countrymen are right when they say that he is still alive today, for he won so much praise that, although he is dead, his name lives on. Who follows his example is always well protected from shameful disgrace.

There was a learned knight who read books and, whenever he had nothing better to do, devoted himself to composing such things as people like to hear. He was Hartmann von Aue and the one who put this tale into verse.

For Whitsuntide King Arthur, in his usual splendid manner, arranged the most magnificent festival in his castle at Karidol that he ever had, before or since. An ordinary man truly amounted to nothing there, because never before had so many noble knights gathered at any place on earth. And their life at the court was in every way all that one could wish: many of the most beautiful maidens and ladies in the country made their visit pleasant. I am really troubled and, if it would help, would complain loudly that there can't be such a joyful occasion in our day as back then. But we, too, have advantages. I wouldn't want to have lived at that time instead of now, when we can get so much delight from hearing about them, whereas they had only their own deeds to enjoy.

Both Arthur and the queen strove to meet the wishes of everyone. After the Whitsuntide meal each sought out the pleasures which suited him best. Some chatted with the ladies; some went walking; some danced and sang; some competed in footraces, leaping, or spear throwing; some listened to string music; some told sad love stories; some talked of heroic deeds. Gawein was looking over his weapons; Keii had lain down to sleep amid the people in the hall: comfort, not honor, concerned him. The king and queen had walked hand in hand to a room and gone to bed, more because of love than of languor. Soon both went to sleep. Outside by the wall sat four knights: Dodines, Gawein, Segremors, and Iwein. The uncouth Keii was also there (lying down), and a sixth knight, Kalogrenant, was beginning to tell them of an incident that had caused him a great deal of trouble without increasing his fame. He had hardly started when the queen awoke and heard him talking. She left her husband in bed and stole away, approaching them so quietly that no one noticed her until she was close by, suddenly standing right in their midst. Their surprise was such that only Kalogrenant sprang up at once, bowed, and greeted her. At this Keii again showed his usual nature. He was vexed that the man had had this honor and therefore spoke very scornfully to him, trying to belittle it.

"Sir Kalogrenant," he said, "we knew very well even before that none of us was so courtly and well bred as you fancy you are. We shall let you win the contest since you think you deserve to more than all your comrades. My lady, too, must concede this or do you an injustice, for your manners are in every respect so fine and you believe yourself to be so perfect. But truly you don't know what you have presumed for yourself today. None of us was so sluggish but that he would have shown the same manners as you if he had seen the queen. And since we didn't move, because we didn't see her or for any other reason, you also could have remained seated."

The queen answered him, saying, "Keii, that is just your nature—never wanting to see another person honored in any way—and you harm no one by it but yourself. You spare nei-

ther retinue nor guests with your envy. For you the most
worthless person is the best, and the best is the most worthless. But I can give you some words of cheer: they will always put up with you because of your habit of excusing all
the rogues and venting your ill temper only on good men. To
sensible people your abuse is praise. If you hadn't said this,
you surely would have burst, which, God knows, would have
been a good thing, since you are full of a caustic poison in
which your heart floats and works to your shame."

Keii did not accept the rebuke. "Lady," he spoke, "that is
enough, indeed, too much. And it would have been more
fitting to your position if you had said less. As is proper, I
am gladly subject to your rule and correction, but it goes too
far. You insult knights. We have not been used to this from
you, and it demeans you. You scold me as if I were a boy.
Forbearance is better than justice, and you could have left
me alone since I have done nothing to you. If my offense
were any greater, it could have cost me my life. Lady, be
merciful and not so angry, because your wrath is too harsh.
Don't give up your kindly manner because of me, since I will
endure the reproach if you will say no more. If I was wrong,
I would be glad to have his pardon. Now ask him for your
sake to finish the story he had begun, because one is accus-
tomed to being silent in your presence."

Kalogrenant answered him thus: "Your nature is such
that one should never pay any attention if you are critical. I
know this: a man's lips speak only as his heart teaches, and
when your tongue is insulting, it is the fault of your heart.
There are many false and inconstant men in the world who
would like to be upright, but their hearts won't let them.
Whoever tries to teach you wastes his time because you
won't change your habits for anyone: bumblebees sting,
hornets buzz, and dung stinks wherever it is. I wouldn't be
pleased with your praise and friendship, since your words
mean nothing, and you won't harm me, no matter how you
rail. You have maligned better men; why should you spare
me? But I am not going to tell a story, now or at any other
time when you are present. May my lady be so kind as to
excuse me."

"Well, don't make these lords pay for my fault," spoke Sir Keii, "since they did nothing to you. My lady should insist on your relating the tale because it would not be right for the rest to be deprived along with me." Then the good queen said, "Sir Kalogrenant, you have grown up with his bad manners and know very well that they have often disgraced him and that nobody pays any attention to his derision. It is my wish and my will that you tell your story, for he would be happy if he kept us from hearing it."

"Your wish is my command," replied Kalogrenant. "Since you will not let me off, then all of you should reward me by listening politely. I shall give my account the more willingly if you are attentive. Many words are to no purpose if one does not keep still and pay attention. Some lend their ears, but if they do not understand with their hearts, it is only sound. And that is too bad, for both he who speaks and those who hear are merely wasting time. You may listen all the more readily because what I tell is true. I know, since it happened to me.

"About ten years ago I rode into the forest of Breziljan, armed as usual and seeking *aventiure*. There were several roads, and I took one to the right, which soon became narrow and overgrown, I rode all day through brambles and thickets: indeed, I can truly say that I never had such a difficult journey. Toward evening I found a path which led me out of the wilderness to open country. I followed it for some four miles until I saw a castle and turned toward it in hope of receiving food and shelter. I rode toward the gate, in front of which was a knight who was holding a falcon on his hand. It was the lord of the castle, and when he saw me riding toward him from a distance, he did not wait but came and took my reins and held my stirrup for me even before I had time to finish my greeting. Having seized me thus, he welcomed me in a most friendly manner. May God forever reward him!

"Before the gate hung a gong from two chains. He struck it so that it rang out and resounded into the castle, and shortly afterwards the lord's attendants—handsome young knights and squires, dressed according to their station—sprang forth and greeted me. My horse and I were well cared for. And when I entered the castle, a young lady soon came and received me. I still say what I said then, that I never saw a more beautiful girl. She helped me off with my armor, and I have only one complaint, which should surprise no one: there are so few straps that she didn't have to spend a long time at it. She finished too quickly; I wouldn't have minded if it had gone on forever. She put a cloak of fine wool on me, unlucky man. Why did I ever meet her, since we had to part!

"During the time we two were alone, the lovely girl could see that I enjoyed being with her, so she led me a little apart from the other people to the finest lawn in the world. God knows I was pleased at this, for I found in her great beauty and every virtue. She sat cordially beside me, listened to what I said, and responded in a friendly manner. Neither maiden nor woman had ever before so captured my heart and troubled my spirit, and probably none ever shall again. Oh, how downcast I was when a messenger came from my host, who asked us to come to eat, for I had to break off our pleasant talk. When I went to dinner with her, the lord of the castle welcomed me once more. Never did a host show more honor to a guest. Again and again he blessed the roads which led me there and even went so far as not to separate the girl and me, but kindly allowed us to eat together. Care was also taken that we had plenty of everything needed for a feast. They served us fine food with willing hands.

"While we were sitting together, after having finished an enjoyable meal, I told the lord that I was riding in search of *aventiure*. This surprised him greatly, and he said that never before had one of his guests claimed to have such a quest. He asked that I do him the honor of stopping over with him on my way back. I could not object to that: I made a promise and later kept it. At bedtime I remembered my journey, and since I neither would nor should remain longer, I thanked the noble girl for her kindness. The charming young creature laughed and thanked me in return, and then I had to leave her. I commended the retinue to God and took leave of my host with many words of gratitude. Very early in the morning I departed and rode from the open country back into the forest.

"I hurried toward the wilderness and in the late morning found a clearing which showed no signs of human habitation. There, to my distress, I saw something frightful: a savage battle of all the kinds of animals of which I had ever heard. Aurochs and bison struggled there with frightful roars. I stopped and regretted having come, because if they had seen me, I could not have hoped to defend myself except by praying to God to save me. Then I saw a man sitting in their midst, which reassured me. But when I came nearer and looked at him closely, I was as much afraid of him as of the beasts, or even more. His form, though human, was indeed strange. He was black, huge, and unbelievably horrible. His head was truly larger than that of an aurochs, and the bristly black hair of his scalp and beard was completely matted to the skin. His face was a yard wide and furrowed with deep wrinkles, and his ears, large as mangers, were overgrown with hair a span long, like those of a wood sprite. The mustache and eyebrows of the hideous man were long, shaggy, and gray. The nose was short, broad, covered with hair, and the size of an ox's. The face was bony and flat—oh, how frightful he appeared! The eyes were red and angry-looking, and the mouth—which extended almost from ear to ear—had great teeth, more like a boar's than a man's. They jutted forth out of his mouth: long, harp, and wide. His matted chin seemed to have grown to his chest, and his back arched up to a hump. He wore unusual clothing—two hides, stripped from some animals just recently—and carried such a huge club that I felt uncomfortable near him.

"When I rode close enough for him to see me clearly, he stood up quickly and came toward me. I couldn't tell whether his intentions were hostile or friendly and was ready to defend myself. Neither of us spoke. When he remained silent, I thought he might be mute and so I asked a question: 'Are you a foe or a friend?' 'I am a friend of him who means me no harm,' he answered.

" 'Can you say what sort of creature you are?'

" 'I'm a man, as you see.'

" 'What do you do here?'

" 'I take care of these animals.'

" 'Tell me, do they ever attack you?'

" 'They are glad enough when I don't do anything to them.'

" 'Are they really afraid of you?'

" 'I watch them, and they fear me as their lord and master.'

" 'But tell me, how do your oversight and mastery prevent them from running off into forest and field whenever they wish? For they are, after all, wild beasts, which are subject neither to man nor to his command. I wouldn't have thought that anyone but God Himself had the power to control them without chains or fetters.' 'My voice and my hand,' he replied, 'my command and my threat, have tamed them so that they tremble before me and do my will. But anyone else would be lost at once if he walked among them as I do.'

"Sir, if they are afraid of your anger, then order them to leave me alone.' 'Have no fear,' he answered, 'they won't hurt you while I am here. Now, I have told you all you wanted to know, so you shouldn't object to saying what it is you are seeking. If there is anything you want of me, I will do it.' 'I'll tell you,' I said, 'I am looking for *aventiure.*' '*Aventiure,*' replied the monster, 'what is that?'

" 'I'll explain it to you. See how I am armed. I am called a knight, and my purpose is to ride in search of a man who is armed like me and will fight with me. He will gain fame by defeating me, while if I win the victory, I shall be thought a valiant warrior and be esteemed more highly. If you should happen to know of a place nearby where such combat is to be found, do not conceal it from me but direct me there, because that is just what I am seeking.'

" 'I never heard of anything like this *aventiure,*' he answered, 'but since you are looking for hardship and don't want peace and comfort, I'll tell you something; and if you want to risk your life, you don't need to ask further. Not more than three short leagues from here is a spring. If you go there, treat it in the right manner, and return without being put to shame, I shall not doubt that you are indeed a brave man. I don't need to say more because if you aren't timid, you'll soon find out everything for yourself. However, let me tell you about the spring. There is a pretty little chapel beside it, and it is cold and clear. Neither rain nor sun touches it, and the winds do not trouble its surface, all because of a linden tree, the most beautiful one ever seen. It provides shade and a roof, for it is so broad and high and has such dense foliage that neither the rain nor the sun's rays come through. And the winter has no effect on its beauty since it keeps its leaves the year round. Above the spring is a splendidly carved stone with many holes in it that is supported by four marble animals, while a vessel of the finest gold hangs from a limb by a silver chain. All you need to do, if you are not afraid, is to take the vessel and pour some water from the spring onto the stone: if you leave there then with honor, you will indeed be lucky.'

"The wild man showed me a path to the left, which I took and learned that he had told the truth, for I found wondrous things. As long as the world lasts no one will ever again hear such splendid bird song as I heard when riding up to the linden tree: a man who was dying of sorrow would have become happy there. The linden was so covered with birds that I could see neither limbs nor leaves. No two were alike, and their melodies—some high-pitched, some low—were all different. How song answered song as the notes echoed loudly from the forest! I saw the spring and everything of which the wild man had spoken. The stone was an emerald, and from each of its corners a ruby gleamed so brightly that the morning star is not more beautiful as it rises above the mist.

"When I caught sight of the hanging vessel, I thought at once that it would be cowardly not to try it, since I was riding in search of *aventiure*. And so my folly, which often gets me into trouble, led me to pour water on the stone. The bird song was still, and the sun, which had been shining brightly, disappeared with the approach of a fierce storm. Clouds gathered from every direction, and the clear day became so dark that I could barely make out the linden. Very soon I saw all around me a thousand thousand flashes of lightning, followed by as many thunderclaps of such violence that I fell to the ground. It rained and hailed: God's grace alone saved me from death. The frightful tempest broke down the forest, and those trees large enough to withstand it were as stripped of leaves as if they had been burned. All living things that didn't flee quickly died at once. Because of the storm's fury, I gave up hope and expected to die, and doubtless would have except that in a short time the hail and wind ceased, and it began to get light again.

"After the weather improved and the danger was past, I truly could have spent ten years beside the spring without pouring water on it. I would have done better to have refrained the first time. The birds returned, their feathers again covering the linden, and raised their sweet voices to sing much better than before. I now forgot all my distress and felt as if in paradise: my joy was the greatest I have ever known. Carefree, I fancied I would have happiness without sorrow from then on. But see how this thought deceived me, for shame and grief were approaching.

"Now look at the knight there. He rode up in a manner so fierce and stern that it seemed like an army coming, but I got ready to fight. He was large and rode a powerful horse, which was bad for me, and his voice rang out like a horn, so I could readily tell that he was angry. However, when I saw that he was alone, my fear and concern were calmed. I thought I would live through it all right and tightened the saddle girth. By the time I mounted, he was close enough to see me, and when he did, he called out loudly from a distance: 'Treacherous knight, you have arrogantly done me an insulting injury without having declared a feud. Look at my forest! You have destroyed it, killed the animals, and driven away the wild fowl. I declare myself your enemy, and if I live, you'll pay for this. The child who has been struck does well to cry and accuse. With like right I accuse you, for I have never knowingly done you any harm and have suffered great loss without cause. There will be no more peace here. Defend yourself if you value your life.'

"As he was larger than I, I told him I wasn't to blame and sought to win his good will. However, he said only that I'd better fight if I wanted to save myself. So I did what I could, which didn't help: I jousted with him and lost my horse. The best I could do was to break my spear against him, while he threw me so neatly on the ground behind my horse that I quite forgot I had been mounted. He left me lying there and took my horse. However, what vexed me most was that he didn't even do me the honor of looking at me, but when he had won, acted just as if he did this ten times a day. His was the fame and mine the shame. Still, I shouldn't be blamed for what happened, because my intent was the best: I just couldn't carry it out and had to fail.

"Since my horse was gone and I couldn't lie there forever, I thought it well to leave on foot and went, as one disgraced, to sit down again at the spring. As curious as I usually am, you should not think me so ill-mannered as to sprinkle it again. Once was enough. I sat there for a rather long time, considering what to do, for my armor was too heavy to walk in. Well, what else can I tell you? I took it off and started out. I did not know where to turn in this wretched state until my heart counseled me to go to my host whom I had left that morning. On my arrival I was received no differently than the evening before when I was mounted. Such was his courtesy. He treated me as well as if he had seen me returning triumphant instead of humbled. Thus did he and the girl console me. May God forever bless them! I have never before told this story of my shame and was foolish not to keep on being still about it; but if something better had happened to me, I would tell you that also. Whichever one of you has been more fortunate there can say so now if he chooses."

Sir Iwein, who was related to him, spoke up: "Cousin Kalogrenant, I, too, want to go and see the spring and its wonders, and my hand shall avenge you." Then Keii said something which was quite like him, for he couldn't help being offended when anyone else excelled. "It's very clear, God knows," he spoke, "that these words were said after dinner, and I can hear indeed that you didn't fast. One mug of wine, I tell you, yields more bravery and boasting than forty-four of water or beer. When the cat has eaten its fill, it feels playful, just as you do, Sir Iwein. Take my advice: your words are too rash. Sleep on it a little, and if you have a bad

dream, you can be more restrained. If not, go your way with
God's blessing, and you need not share with me either the
honors or the misfortune that will be yours."

"Sir Keii," said the queen, "shame on your tongue, which
never says anything good, only the worst things you can
think of. But I suppose that I do it an injustice, because it is
forced to this by your heart, for which no malice is too great:
the tongue speaks as the heart directs. Still, I can't separate
them and so I condemn them both. I tell you truly, if you
killed a man's father, he would be no more eager to rob you
of all honor than your tongue is. If you alone suffer because
of it, that serves you right." Sir Iwein just laughed and said,
"Lady, I don't mind what Sir Keii tells me. I know very well
that he is only rebuking me for being stupid. He is annoyed
at my crudeness and simply can't overlook it. Moreover, he
understands how to reprove me: with his usual tact, which
indeed can offend no one. Sir Keii is so wise, so famous, and
so respected that one must be glad to listen to him. You
know that I'm right. Moreover, the man who strikes out does
not start a dispute if the other lets it go, for then the quarrel
is over. I don't want to be like the dog that growls back
whenever another dog snarls." A great deal of such mockery
followed.

Meanwhile, the king, too, had slept his fill. When he
awoke, he got up and came out at once to where they were
sitting together. They sprang to their feet, which vexed him
because of his friendship to them: God knows he acted much
more as their comrade than as their lord. He sat down, and
the queen told him of Kalogrenant's misfortune and all the
rest of the story. Now, it was the king's custom never to swear
by the soul of his father, Uterpandragon, without keeping
his oath in full. He swore by him on the spot—and had it
proclaimed far and wide—that in two weeks, right on St.
John's Eve, he would ride to the spring with his entire court.
Everyone thought this knightly and good when they heard
it, for all wanted to go there. But in spite of their joy, Sir
Iwein was displeased, as he had decided to go alone. He
thought, "If the king does this, I shall lose my chance for
knightly combat, because I can't prevent Sir Gawein from

getting ahead of me. As soon as he asks for the contest, it will be granted to him before me: there is no doubt of that. But truly it will be different. I can very easily keep anyone who waits for two weeks from fighting before I do, because I shall set out secretly within three days and search the forest of Breziljan until I find the narrow, overgrown path which Kalogrenant came upon. And then I shall see the beautiful girl and her father, the noble lord of the castle, both of whom are so courtly. When I leave there, I shall see the ugly man who takes care of the animals and, soon afterward, the stone and the spring. They cannot stop me from sprinkling it by myself, whether, for pain or pleasure. No one will hear of this until I have done it, and it will be all right when they find out afterward."

So he stole away—just like a man who knew how to win and preserve honor by being clever—and went to where the squires were. He quickly chose the best and concealed nothing from him. Very secretly he told him to saddle his horse and said that he would ride forth and wait at a distance for the squire to bring him his armor. "Now hurry," he spoke, "and see that you keep quiet about it, because, truly, if you tell anyone, our friendship is over forever." He rode out, leaving the squire behind, and soon afterward the latter brought him his armor and his battle steed. He armed himself at once, mounted, and rode on at random. With great toil he searched over a broad wilderness, through field and forest, until he found the narrow path along which his cousin, Kalogrenant, had barely been able to force his way. He, too, had a great deal of trouble before he came out into open country and found the fine lodging: no host had ever made him so comfortable for the night. He departed the next morning and came upon the frightful man in a field, standing beside his wild beasts. At the sight of him, he crossed himself many times in wonderment that it had ever pleased God to form such a creature. The latter directed him to that which he sought.

Sir Iwein soon saw the tree, the spring, and the stone and heard the songs of the birds. Without delay he poured water on the stone. There was a rushing and roaring, followed by a

storm so fierce that he thought he had been too hasty, for he
didn't expect to live through it. When it was over, he heard
the galloping of the lord of the forest, who greeted him from
a distance as an enemy: it was quite clear to Sir Iwein that
he had to defend himself or endure shame and distress. Each
man was determined to defeat his opponent. Eager and
angry, they spurred their steeds in their haste to get at each
other, and each thrust his spear through the shield and
against the mail of the other so fiercely that the shaft broke
in a hundred pieces. Then they drew swords, and a battle
began which God Himself could have watched with respect if
it had taken place before Him. The shields the knights held
in front of them suffered greatly while they lasted and were
soon so chopped up as to be useless.

I could make a great deal out of the battle, but will not
because they were alone and no one else was there to con-
firm my words. Should I describe it when nobody saw how
this one slashed and that one stabbed? One of them was
killed there—he couldn't tell of it—and the victor was such a
courtly man that he would not have wanted to say much
about his bravery. I could, therefore, very well limit the force
and number of their strokes and thrusts except to tell you
that neither was faint-hearted, for many blows were exchanged before the intruder cut through the helmet of the
lord of the land, deep down to the seat of life itself. When
the latter felt the mortal wound, it was the pain of death,
rather than cowardice, which made him turn and flee. For-
getting his courtly manners, Sir Iwein pursued him toward
his castle. The half-dead man bent his whole will to flight,
and his steed was so swift that he almost escaped. It then
occurred to Sir Iwein that, if he did not capture or slay him,
it would turn out as Sir Keii—who spared no one his
scorn—had predicted. What good would all his efforts do him
since there was no witness—no one was there—and Keii
would deprive him of any fame. He therefore chased after
the lord with such speed that the hoofbeats of their horses
rang out together until the castle came into view.

Now, the castle road was not wide enough for two, and
they had to go along a narrow defile to approach the main

gate, at the entrance to which hung a portcullis. One had to pass through here and needed to watch out very carefully in order not to be killed. If either horse or man stepped in the wrong place, this would move the catch which held up the massive portcullis, and it would fall so quickly that no one could leap out of the way. It was so heavy and sharp that it would cut through iron and bone: many a man had died thus. The castle's lord rode in first and he knew just where to go to avoid mishap, for he was the one who had had it built there. Sir Iwein did not know he should beware of it and caused the portcullis to drop, but at that very instant, he hit and wounded the lord and was not killed. I'll tell you how it was. In order to strike the blow, he had leaned forward, which saved his life, for when the portcullis fell, it missed him although (as I have heard) it cut his steed in two at the saddle and sliced away his sword sheath and both spurs from his heels. He was lucky to escape. When his steed fell dead, he could not keep up the chase. But he had given a mortal wound to the lord, who fled on beneath a second portcullis, which he let fall behind him so that the intruder could go neither forward nor back. My Sir Iwein was, therefore, caught and locked in between these two portals. Still, however badly things had turned out—with his imprisonment—his chief regret was that the man had gotten away alive.

I'll tell you about the castle in which he was trapped. It was more splendid, as he said later, than any he had seen before or since: tall, broad, strongly built, and painted all over with gold. Whoever had been in it without cause for fear would have thought it delightful.

Iwein looked all around without finding either window or door from which to escape, and then began to wonder what should be done. Not long after he had started to worry about this, a small door opened near him, and he saw coming out to him a girl who would have been beautiful if her face had not been marred by grief. At first she said only, "Oh! Oh! Your coming here, knight, will soon cost you your life, for you have killed my lord. So piteous is the lamenting and so fierce the anger of my lady and the court that you must die.

Only the weeping for my lord has put off your death, but they will slay you soon." "I'll not lose my life like a woman," he said. "They won't find me defenseless." "May God protect you," she replied. "Only He can do so, otherwise you must die. Still, no one ever conducted himself better in great danger. You are brave all right and should be rewarded for it. In spite of the grief you have caused me, I don't hate you and I'll tell you why.

"My lady once sent me to Brittany, where I delivered a message from her to the king. Sir, believe me, I might have left there without a single person speaking to me. I now know that it was because of my uncourtly behavior, since—according to the customs there—I had acted in such a way as not to deserve a greeting from them. I paid for it: you spoke to me, sir, but no one else. I shall reward you now for the respect you showed me then. I know who you are, sir: your father was King Urien. Sir Iwein, take this ring and you will be safe from harm. The stone is of such a nature that whoever holds it in his bare hand cannot be seen or found as long as he keeps it there. You don't need to worry any longer: you will be hidden like wood under bark." So she gave it to him. There was a couch close by that was as splendid as could be: no king ever had a better. She told him to sit down and, when he had done so, asked, "Would you like something to eat?" "Yes indeed," he replied, "I would be grateful to you." She left and soon returned carrying a fine and ample cold lunch, for which he thanked her. After he had eaten and drunk, there arose a great tumult at both portals from the courtiers, who intended to take revenge on the one who had slain their lord.

"Do you hear, Sir Iwein?" the girl asked. "They have come for you. Now do as I say and stay on the couch, for no less than your life is at stake. Close your hand on the stone I gave you, and I'll pledge my soul that you won't be harmed, because truly no one will see you. What could be better? You will see all your enemies standing near you and going around you with ready weapons and yet so blinded that they can't find you even though you are right in their midst. His dear friends will also carry my lord past you on a bier when

they take him to be buried. Then, indeed, they will search
for you everywhere, but you don't need to worry about it.
Just do as I say and you will be safe. But I can't stay with
you any longer, for it could be bad for us if they found me
here." With this she departed.

The people who came to the outer portcullis saw half a
horse in front of it and were certain that they would find the
rider inside when the gate was open—no one could have persuaded them otherwise. They quickly opened both portals
and found no one there, only half a horse—from the saddle
forward—lying inside the portcullis. Then they began to rave
with anger and thanked neither God nor the devil. "Where is
the man?" they cried. "Or has someone robbed us of sight
and senses? He must be in here. With seeing eyes we are all
blind. Everyone here can see well, and no living thing larger
than a mouse could have gotten out as long as this gate was
closed. So how did the man elude us? But though he may
protect himself for a while with magic tricks, we'll surely
find him, and today. Look in the corners, good friends, and
under the benches. Then he can't hide and will have to appear." They blocked the entrances and went about, swinging
their swords in all directions like blind men; they couldn't be
stopped from this. If it had been at all possible for them to
find him, they indeed would have. They even looked under
the couch. I must conclude from Sir Iwein's escape that any
trick will save a man as long as he is not destined to die.

While he was anxiously sitting there, everything took
place that his friend, the kindly girl, had foretold. He saw
the lord whom he had slain being carried toward him and,
walking behind the bier, the most beautiful woman he had
ever seen. She was tearing her hair and clothing with grief.
No woman in the world could have been more wretched, for
she was looking at the dead body of one of the dearest men a
woman ever loved. And no woman who was not greatly distressed could have caused herself such pain while lamenting.
Both her voice and her actions showed deep sorrow. Her
grief was so frenzied that the bright day often became night
for her as she fainted. When she opened her eyes again, she
could not speak or listen, and her hands spared neither her

hair nor her headdress. Sir Iwein caught glimpses of her bare form, and her hair and body were so beautiful that love robbed him of reason, to the point that he quite forgot himself and almost left his seat when she tore her hair and beat herself. He could hardly endure it and wanted to go and hold her hands to keep her from striking herself any more. He was so distressed by the pain of the lovely woman that he would rather have suffered it himself and lamented to God the misfortune that she should meet with any sorrow because of him. Her misery moved him until he would rather have died than see her hurt a finger.

One thing has often been told us as true: a slain man will bleed again when he is borne past the one who killed him, no matter how long he may have been dead. Now look! The lord's wounds began to bleed as they carried him into the hall, for he was near his slayer. Seeing this, the lady cried out loudly: "He is in here and has cast a spell on our senses." Then those who had given up the search began anew. The couch was cut up, many thrusts and slashes passed through the quilt on it, and Iwein often had to dodge. They sought him in corners and under benches with their swords, as eager for his death as the wolf for that of the sheep. They were beside themselves with rage. The lady began to quarrel with God, saying, "Lord, I have lost my husband in a very strange manner, and You alone are to blame. You gave him such strength and courage that he could never fail against natural forces. It could only happen this way: it was an invisible spirit that killed him. Lord God, his death must have been ordained, for You know well that he could have defended himself easily against anyone but a sorcerer. This one is among us and listening. See how brave he is! Since he was bold enough to kill my lord, why is he too timid to let a woman see him? What could she do to him?"

After they had searched for some time and Sir Iwein's stone had protected him from harm—because no one could see him—they stopped looking and carried the dead man to the cathedral, where there was a funeral mass with prayers and the lawful dispensing of alms. Then, amid mournful cries of deep grief, he was borne to the grave. Soon afterward

the girl stole away from the retinue to see the hidden knight
and console him as a courtly maiden well may. But he was
not downcast, because love had raised his spirits—as it often
does—and he had no fear of death. Still he did not tell the
girl of his great love for his enemy. "How can I get to see
her?" he thought.

Now, the place where the lord was buried was close
enough for the knight to hear the lamenting as clearly as if
he were among the mourners. He therefore spoke slyly: "Oh,
these people are very sad, and their sorrow moves me more
than I can say. If it were possible, I would like to witness the
grief of those I hear at the grave." However, he didn't mean
it, for he would not have cared a straw if the entire court
had died and was lying here on biers as long as the lady still
lived. He was quite troubled to hear and not see her until, at
his request, the girl comforted him by opening a window
over his head, which allowed him to look at the lady. He saw
her in great distress because of her grief. "Dear companion,"
she cried, "with you has died the bravest and most generous
knight who ever lived: no one was ever such a model of
knighthood. Oh, I don't know why or how you were taken
from me! Death could atone for all he has done to me if he
granted my request to depart with you now. How can I get
along without you! What good are wealth and life? What
shall I do, unhappy woman that I am? Oh, that I was ever
born! Oh, how did I lose you? Oh, my loved one! May God protect
you from hell with His power and give you the company of the
angels, for you were always the best of men." And she tore her
hair and clothing in anguish.

When Sir Iwein beheld this, he ran to the entrance, since
he wanted to hurry out and hold her hands. Seeing what he
was about to do, the girl drew him back and said, "Tell me,
where do you want to go and where did you get such an
idea? There are many people in front of the gate who are
very angry at you. You will die if you don't listen to me."
Her rebuke restrained him. "What got into you?" she continued. "If this notion had been carried out, it would have
gone badly with you. I can't hope to save your life if you
don't want me to. For God's sake, just sit still! It is a wise

man who can put an end to foolish whims with sensible
deeds, but he whose mind is such that he wants to act on
every idle thought is wrong most of the time. If some folly
occurs to you, put it aside, but if you have a clever idea,
carry it out—that's the thing to do. Sir, I must leave you
alone and go back at once to the courtiers because I am
afraid they might find out that I have come to you. If they
miss me, they will soon get suspicious." She went away and
left him there.

Although the power of love had captured his mind, he still
remembered one misfortune: that he could not disarm the
mockery he would encounter at court when he could not
produce any visible proof of his success and that, therefore,
all his trouble would be for nothing. He was afraid of the ill
nature of Keii, who, he knew, would never spare him scorn
and spite. These two cares brought him like pain at first, but
soon one began to trouble him more, as Lady Love got the
upper hand, seizing and binding him. She attacked him with
a greater force and compelled him to fall deeply in love with
a deadly enemy. The latter had been avenged on him more
than she knew, for he was mortally wounded: by the hand of
Lady Love. Such a wound is said to fester longer than that
from a sword or a spear because whoever is wounded by a
weapon heals quickly if his doctor is at hand, but this wound
is deadly and causes ever growing distress just when the
only doctor who could treat it is near.

Love had been spreading herself over many a poor place
where she had not been invited, so that little was gained,
but now she had come here with all her might in order that
her dominion would be the more complete. One thing is re-
grettable: although Love is so strong that she captures
whomever she wishes and subdues all the kings alive more
easily than a child, she is still vulgar in that she has always
lowered herself to the extent of desiring that which is common and seeking out trifling places that should have been
too mean and petty for her. In spite of her charm, she has
often fallen under the feet of shame, like one who pours his
sweet honey into bile and lets balsam—which also could
have found better use—flow from his hand into the ashes.

But this time Love did nothing amiss, and we shall not find
fault. She chose here a host who will never demean or disgrace her. She stopped at the right place and can stay here
with honor. She should always take such lodgings.

After the lord was buried, his grieving subjects departed,
each returning to his own affairs, while the lady remained at
the grave, alone with her sorrow. When Sir Iwein saw her by
herself with her great trouble, her bitter anger, her constant
goodness, her wifely loyalty, and her longing sadness, he
loved her all the more and felt such desire for her that Lady
Love never gained greater power over any man. He thought
to himself, "Oh, good Lord God, who is stirring up my passion to make me love so painfully a mortal enemy? How
could she be kind to me in spite of my great offense? I know
very well that, having killed her husband, I can never win
her favor. But yet, to give up hope would be too
faint-hearted. I know one thing which can console me: if
Lady Love becomes her mistress as she has become mine,
she will in a short time make an unseemly matter appear
quite proper. It is not impossible. However much she now
hates me, should Love attack her also and order her to be
fond of me, she would have to give up her anger and take me
into her heart even if I had caused her still greater sorrow.
Lady Love must incline her toward me, for I can't hope to
take away her grief on my own merits. It would also be
easier if she knew how I was forced to kill her husband and
if she knew my feelings: that I want to give myself and my
life in exchange for him.

"Since Love has taken possession of me, she rightly should
do one of two things: make the lady well disposed toward me
or let me turn my thoughts away from her; otherwise I am
lost. That I chose a mortal enemy as a sweetheart was not
my doing but Love's, and it would be unjust for her to forsake me. Oh, if only my lady's actions were more in keeping
with her goodness! Happiness and a light heart would suit
her better than self-hate. The pain and distress she inflicts
on herself might better be mine. Oh, what have her beautiful face and body—the likes of which I have never
seen—done to her? I truly don't know what she could be

avenging on her body and golden hair that she should wound herself. She is innocent, for it was I indeed who killed her husband. It would be more just for me to receive this punishment, and she would do better to show God her pain on my body. Oh, why is the charming one, even in her grief, so really wonderful! To whom could one compare her if she were happy? God surely used all his skill and power, his zeal and his mastery on this beauty. She is not a woman, but an angel."

As he sat there in hiding, Sir Iwein was both happy and troubled. He was pleased by the window because he enjoyed watching her, but, on the other hand, he was afraid he might die. And so he felt both joyful and distressed. He sat there looking at her until she went back through the hall and was hardly able to keep from speaking to her as she walked past. However, his fear restrained him. After she had gone through, the portals were closed, blocking the exit and making him again a prisoner. But he didn't mind that, for even if both portals had been opened wide and he had been freed of all guilt and permitted to go where he wished, he still would have had no other desire than to stay there. If he had been someplace else, he would have wanted to return, for his heart would remain only where she was: that was the best spot for him.

Sir Iwein was thus sorely oppressed by these two cares: although he had succeeded, he would have been laughed at if he had returned to the court without proof of his story, for it would not have been believed; on the other hand, he was assailed by the feeling that whatever honor he might receive would be nothing to him if he could not see the lady who had taken him captive. Soon the friendly girl who was helping him returned. "I suppose you are having a troublesome and unpleasant time in here," she said. "On the contrary," he replied, "I never spent a happier day."

"Happier day? Tell me, sir, how can that be? You have seen people walking all around you who would like to kill you. Can a man who does not long for death have a good, easy time when he is a prisoner whose life is in danger?" "I certainly don't want to die," was the answer, "yet I am happy in spite of the danger and hope also for future happiness."

He was only half finished when the clever girl knew that he was thinking of her lady, as she later told him. She said, "You may well rejoice, for I shall arrange one way or another to get you away secretly either today or tomorrow morning." "If I were to leave here by stealth and on foot," he replied, "it would bring me nothing but scorn and disgrace. When I leave here, the whole country will know it." She took him by the hand, saying, "Truly, I am not telling you to go anywhere, and I shall gladly protect you as best I can. Now, Sir Iwein, come to where you will be safer." And she led him to a place nearby where everything needful was done for him. She provided him with all the comforts his body required and such good care that he quite recovered from the rigors of the day. When this was done, she left him and with the best of intentions, for she was fully resolved that he should become the master there.

She went straight to her mistress, with whom she was so intimate that she shared all her secrets and was her closest and best friend. The lady took her advice more than that of all the other ladies in waiting. The girl said, "One may indeed see your goodness in that you bear your grief as is right and proper. You lament as a woman should and perhaps even more. Our slain lord was an excellent man; may God now help you get another like him."

"Are you serious?"

"Yes, my lady."

"But where?"

"There is one somewhere."

"You are mad or joking. If God did His very best, He could never create a better man. And therefore, God willing, I'll mourn him until I die. I hope God sends death quickly so that I may follow my lord at once. You will lose my favor if you ever praise another as highly as him: you would have to be mad."

To this the girl replied, "Whether you take it amiss or not, I still must remind you of one thing. Your state is simply this: if you do not wish to lose your spring, your land, and the respect of others, you must choose someone to defend the spring for you because many more brave knights will come and seize control of it, should there be no one to protect it. Moreover, there is something you don't know: a messenger to my lord just came. When he found him dead and you in such distress, he said nothing to you but instead asked me to tell you that in twelve days, perhaps sooner, King Arthur and his retinue would arrive at the spring. If there is no one to guard it then, your honor is lost. And should you select a man from your retinue to do this, you'll be misled because, though one of them were to take on the courage of all, he still wouldn't be very brave. Whoever claims to be the best of them wouldn't dare go so far as to defend the spring, for King Arthur is bringing an army of men who are among the most valiant ever born. Therefore, my lady, take warning: if you don't want to lose the spring (and with it the land) without a fight, then you must stop grieving and prepare for its defense in time. I advise this only for your good."

When the lady heard this clear statement of the facts and saw it to be such, she still did as women do: their feelings often make them oppose that which they really think best. A lot of people blame them because many times they do things which before they had rejected, but it seems to me a good custom. He who says it is because they are fickle is wrong. I know why they so often waver back and forth: it comes from their goodness. One can therefore change a false notion of theirs to a right one, but not a right one to a false. Such changes of mind are good and no women have any other. I do not agree with him who says they are inconstant and I speak only well of them. May everything good come to them!

The lady wailed, "I lament to God my grief that I cannot die right now. I'll be sorry to live a single day longer than my husband. If I had a knife or sword and could exchange my life for death without a mortal sin, I would do it at once. If I cannot refuse to replace my husband with another, the world will not understand it as God does: He knows indeed that I surely would not do it if I could give peace to my land by myself. Now advise me, dear, on what, if anything, can be done. Since I can't keep my land peaceful without a brave

man, I'll be glad to find one—only one whom I know to be so
brave that he can protect it—but I won't marry him." "That
can't be," replied the girl. "Who would ever go to such great
trouble for you if he were not your husband? You talk just
like a woman. Even if you gave him both your wealth and
yourself, you could feel lucky if he were willing to do this.
Now you have youth and beauty, noble birth, wealth, and
many virtues and, God willing, can get another husband as
good as the first. Just stop weeping and think of your honor,
my lady, for truly the need is great. Only my lord has died.
Do you think all bravery was buried with him? That is indeed not true, for there are a hundred knights who are better with sword, shield, and spear than he was."

"That is not so."

"Lady, I am telling the truth."

"Then show me one of them."

"If you were to stop crying, I would find him for you easily
enough."

"I don't know what to do with you, for it doesn't seem
possible to me. God help you if you lie to me now and get
pleasure from deceiving me."

"Lady, if I have lied to you, I have betrayed myself, because I have always been with you and my welfare depends
on yours. What would happen to me if I misled you? Now,
you be the judge. Even though you are a woman, you can decide this: when two men engage in mortal combat, who is
the best warrior, the victor or he who lies defeated on the
field?"

"The victor, I guess."

"Lady, it isn't guesswork, it's the plain truth, and a man
defeated my lord just like that. You can't deny it, because
you buried him. He who chased him down and slew him is
the better warrior. My lord is dead and he is alive: that's
proof enough."

The lady was greatly distressed to hear the girl claim that
someone was in any way greater than her lord. She spoke to
her angrily and ordered her to leave at once, saying that she
never wanted to see her again. "I may well suffer for my devotion," said the girl, "but I shall do so gladly and without

regret. I would much rather be driven away because of my loyalty than to remain, knowing I was unfaithful. Lady, I'll leave you now. However, since I've been dismissed, for God's sake consider yourself what might be good and useful for you. I meant well with my advice and only pray that God will grant you honor and good fortune if I do not see you again." With this she stood up and went to the man who was hidden. She brought him bad news—that she could not change the lady's mind, could not persuade her to do what was best, and had gained only anger and threats—all of which made Sir Iwein unhappy. He and the girl began to discuss better means of trying in a friendly manner to change the lady's hate to a more gentle mood.

When the lady had driven the girl away and was alone, she began to regret deeply that she had rewarded the latter so poorly by scolding and abusing her. "What have I done!" she thought. "I am sure she gave me that advice only because of her devotion and I should have remembered that she has served me well. I have never suffered from following her counsel, and she also told the truth just now. I have known her a long time—she is faithful and good—and it was wrong to dismiss her. I could curse my irate conduct: no one gains anything but shame and harm by such behavior. It would be better for me if I had her come back, for I was angry at her without cause. My husband was indeed a brave man, but the one who killed him must be a greater warrior; otherwise he could not have chased him back here. She was right about that. I have good reason to hate whoever killed my husband; yet, to be fair, he is not fully to blame, because he was only defending himself. I could not expect him to be so fond of me that he would spare my husband for my sake and let him have his way. The man would have died himself. He had no choice but to kill him.

In this way she won herself over to kindness and reconciliation and absolved the knight of any wrong to her. Mighty Love, a true mediator between men and women, was there and ready. "I can't defend the spring myself," thought the lady. "A brave man must save me or I am indeed lost. God knows I am willing to give up my anger and, if it can

be, would like to have none other than the man who killed
my husband. If he is in other ways so worthy that I decide to
marry him, then he must make up with devotion for my distress and treat me all the better because of the sorrow he
caused me." She was so sorry to have berated the girl that
she lamented bitterly, and when the girl returned the next
morning, she was received more cordially than she had been
dismissed, which relieved her greatly. The lady had not been
sitting with her very long when she began to ask questions.
"For God's sake, tell me," she said, "who is the man whom
you were praising to me yesterday, the one who killed my
husband? I suppose you weren't out of your mind after all,
for he surely couldn't have been a coward. If he is well born
and young and also has such other good traits as would
make him a suitable husband for me—so that people, when
they hear about it, won't blame me for accepting the man
who slew my lord—and if you can assure me that his many
virtues really will save me from this shameful position, I'll
take him as a husband if that is what you advise."

"I think it a good idea," said the girl, "and am glad for
your sake that you have had so happy a change of mind. You
need never be ashamed of it, because it does you honor."
"Tell me his name," was the reply.

"My lady, it is Sir Iwein." They were in agreement at
once. "He is the son of King Urien," said the lady. "To tell
the truth, I heard of him long ago and can indeed understand everything now. I'll be in luck if he will have me, but,
my friend, do you know for sure that he will?

"He wishes you were already his."

"Tell me, when can I see him?"

"In four days, my lady."

"For God's sake, what are you saying? I can't wait that
long. Find some way for me to see him today or tomorrow."

"How do you expect me to do it, my lady? I can't give you
any hope of that. No man is swift enough to go there and
back in such a short time unless he has wings. You know
how far it is."

"Then do as I say: my page runs fast. He can go as far on
foot in a day as another can ride in two, and the moonlight
will help him so that he can make a day out of the night.

Moreover, the days are now longer than usual. Tell him that I shall always be thankful and he will benefit for a long time if he gets back tomorrow. Say that he is to get his legs moving and turn four days into two. He is to hurry now and later may rest as long as he wishes. Dear friend, urge him to do it."

"I will, my lady," answered the girl, "but there is something else you should do. Send for your thanes today and tomorrow, because you should not take a husband except on their advice. Nothing goes amiss for him who follows good counsel; but if a man does something on his own account and it later turns out badly, he has lost in two ways, for he suffers not only the injury, but also the anger of his friends."

"Oh, I'm afraid it won't go well for me, my dear; maybe they'll be against it."

"Don't worry about that, my lady. You don't have any knight so heroic that he would rather guard the spring for you than let you take whomever you want. Your plan will suit them fine, and they'll be only too glad to be relieved in this manner of having to defend the country. When they hear what you propose, they'll throw themselves at your feet and beg you to take him." "Well, start the page on his way," said the lady, "and I'll send messengers to them so that the matter may be settled."

It didn't take the girl long to get Sir Iwein: he was there at once. The page did as she ordered and hid, since he was just the one for any clever ruse. He could help her lie and deceive as long as no malice was intended. After the lady was led to think that the page was on his way (which was not the case at all), the girl began to get the knight ready. May God reward her! She gave him a bath and brought three kinds of clothing for him—of calabar, of ermine, and of gray and white squirrel—for the lord of the castle had been a courtly man who could afford to dress well and was always supplied with such finery. The girl chose the best and put them on Sir Iwein. The following evening she went to where her lady was sitting alone and caused her both to blanch and to blush with joy. "Reward me as one who brings good tidings," she said, "for your page has returned."

"What news did you hear?"

"Good news."

"Tell me about it."

"Sir Iwein is here, too."

"How could he come so soon?"

"Happiness drove him."

"For God's sake, tell me, who else knows this?"

"No one knows it yet, my lady, but the page and we two."

"Why don't you bring him to me? Go now, and I'll wait here."

When the mischievous girl went to the knight, she acted as if she had been sent with bad news. On seeing him, she hung her head and spoke sadly, "I don't know what to do. My lady knows that you are in the castle and is very angry at me: I have lost her favor by hiding you here. She orders me to bring you to her."

"I want to see her even if it costs my life."

"How could a woman take it?"

"She has a great many subjects."

"You'll be safe indeed without a fight. I have her word that she won't harm you. She only wants to see you alone. You must surrender to her, but you'll be well treated." "She is so lovely," he said, "that I shall be glad for my heart and body to be her prisoners forever."

He stood up and went to the lady, but was received very coldly; she neither spoke nor bowed to him when he came before her. He was greatly troubled by her silence and knew nothing better to do than to sit down at some distance from her and look at her shyly. Since neither said anything, the girl spoke up: "Why are you so timid, Sir Iwein? You are still alive, aren't you, and have a mouth? When did you become a mute? You were speaking just a moment ago. For God's sake, tell me why you are avoiding such a beautiful woman? God damn me forever if I'll pull an unwilling man who can speak very well for himself to a beautiful woman when he doesn't want anything at all to do with her! You could sit a little closer; I'll promise that my lady won't bite you. Whoever causes another such grief as you have caused her should not expect to gain forgiveness so cheaply. You killed her beloved husband, King Ascalon; who would thank you for that? You are the guilty one, and so it is up to you to ask for favor. Let us both beg her to be kind enough to forget the distress she has suffered."

The knight remained seated no longer, but at once threw himself at her feet, as one aware of his guilt, and asked that she receive him kindly. "I can offer you no more in the way of amends and devotion," he said, "than that you should decide my fate: your will shall be my will."

"Will you do anything I say?"

"Yes, nothing would seem too much."

"So I could even take your life."

"I'm at your mercy, charming lady."

"Then we might as well be brief. Since you submit to my power of your own choice, it would be most unwomanly for me to have you slain. Sir Iwein, do not think that it is because of inconstancy that I should quickly forgive you. You have caused me so much sorrow that I would not and should not pardon you with this haste if my situation and possessions were like those of other ladies. But, sad to say, I must hurry, for my plight is such that I can easily lose my land today or tomorrow. Before then I must provide it with a man who will defend it. Since the king was slain, there is no one in my army who is able to do this. I must therefore quickly choose a husband or lose the land. Now please say no more about it. As you have killed my husband, you must indeed be such a brave man that I shall be well protected from the arrogance of strangers if God gives you to me. And, believe me, before I would give you up, I would break with women's custom: although they never ask the man to marry them, I would do so with you. I won't act haughty any longer: I want you; do you want me?"

"Lady, I would be wretched if I said no. This is the happiest day of my life. God grant me the good fortune that we may become man and wife."

"Oh, Sir Iwein," said the queen sorrowfully, "who brought about this love between us? I can't imagine who could have led you to think that I would ever become your wife after the pain you have caused me."

"It was my idea alone."

"But, for God's sake, where did you get it?"

"My heart demanded it."

"And who told your heart?"

"My eyes persuaded it."

"But who advised your eyes?"

"You should be happy to learn that it was no other than your beauty."

"Since each of us is pleased with the other," said the queen then, "who can hinder us from coming to an agreement? Still, this cannot be done by just the three of us, so let us now go to my subjects. Yesterday I sent for the noblest in the land since we dare not conceal the matter from them. I have already let them know something of my intention because it will indeed be best to have them take part in the accord." They did as she proposed.

When the two walked hand in hand into the great hall and the people saw Sir Iwein, they asserted that they had never seen such a splendid man, which was no lie. Moreover, no knight ever was better received anywhere than he was there. They gazed at him as at a marvel, and each asked the other, "Who brought this knight here? God willing, he is the one whom my lady should choose." Never had a knight pleased them so well. When the lady had led him through the midst of her subjects, they sat down together and she bade her lord high steward speak for her: to tell them that she had picked this man and to ask for their approval. They said that they did not object, indeed, that nothing ever suited them better. However eager a horse may be, it still goes a little faster if one spurs it: they had no trouble persuading her to do what was her will and her joy. I think they did right, because if they all had thought it a mistake, she would have taken him anyway.

After the lord high steward spoke as the queen had requested and also told the people that in two weeks King Arthur would arrive with an army—so he had sworn—and that the spring would truly be lost if he found it without a defender, and when they learned of the knight's noble birth and bravery (they had already seen how handsome he was), they maintained, quite correctly, that the marriage would be useful and do them honor. Why say more—everything was just as it should be. There were many priests at hand and they performed the ceremony at once, giving the knight both lady and land.

His wife's name was Laudine, and her attributes were such as to make his life very pleasant, for she was young, highborn, beautiful, and rich. He to whom God has granted loyalty, a noble spirit, and all other good traits (as to Sir Iwein)and also a fine wife who wants only to do his will has been given a great deal of happiness if the two live long and with plenty. Everything was to be hoped for in this case. The wedding festivities began, and the dead man was forgotten as the living one took over honors and land: all became his. A greater celebration was never held in that country before or since. There was splendor and glory, pleasure and knightly sport, and an excess of all one could desire. The contests continued until King Arthur entered the land, as he had sworn to do, and went with his retinue to the spring. It then needed good protection—no coward would have been fitting as its lord—since never before had so many good knights come there at one time.

Sir Keii was happy because he had found an object for his jeers. "Sir Kalogrenant," he said, "where is your cousin, Sir Iwein? It appears now as it did then and, I think, always will: that it was the wine which led him to avenge you here—with words. Oh my, how he slashed and thrust! If he had had another drink, he would have killed twelve giants. What a brave man! But he is pretty late in getting here if he is going to avenge you. I am the one who will do it. I'll just have to face the danger again myself, as I have done so often when I fought for a friend. I don't know why they do it—those who speak so much of their own deeds when no one believes them—or for what they are punishing themselves. It is easy to fight where there is no one to strike back. But now he has slipped away from us, to his own shame. He was afraid that, if he came, he would have to confront the danger because he had said he would. But I would have been glad to let him off and take his place. Many worthless men belittle those who are respected whenever they can. They don't do anything brave themselves, and it pains them if someone else is honored. You see that I don't do that, for I am glad to grant each one his fame: I praise him when he does well and say nothing of his failures, which is right. It is also right that I should succeed, for no one talks less about his exploits than I. But the mean-spirited man helps himself along with self-praise. He has to because no one wants to be so foolish for his sake as to extol his worthlessness. Sir Iwein is not wise: he ought to keep still as I do."

The others thought these words comical: that he should think himself so noble when in fact no knight ever had such a spiteful nature. "How is this, Sir Keii?" spoke then Sir Gawein. "You say you are free of malice. How do you show it? You have just displayed great bitterness toward a fine knight. You wrong him. And he has always thought well of you, as one knight should of another. Some important matter probably hindered him from coming right at this time. For God's sake stop such talk." "All right," replied Sir Keii, "I will, but I think what I said was proper. A man might just as well do evil as good if no one is supposed to talk about it. That is just your kind of honor. However, I won't mention it again."

Since King Arthur wanted to find out whether the story that brought him to the place was true or false, he took the pitcher he saw hanging there, filled it from the spring, and poured water on the stone. At this, such a great storm arose that all who had come got more than they wanted; indeed, they almost despaired of their lives. Then Sir Iwein rode swiftly in full armor down from the castle because he knew very well that if he did not protect his spring, it would be taken away from him. Sir Keii, also armed, waited near the spring, for he wanted the first joust and King Arthur had granted it to him. Sir Iwein soon came galloping out of the forest and onto the field, decked out as splendidly as an angel. Both steed and courage were stalwart and did not fail him. His heart rejoiced when he saw waiting there the one who spoke ill of everything noble and was delighted that God so favored him as to let him repay the man for his coarse insults and constant scorn. He thanked God for this. However, I'll tell you something else: as spiteful as Keii was, he was still very brave. Indeed, if his tongue had not ruined him, the court would not have had a finer hero. You can see this, if you want to, in the position he held. For had he been a coward, King Arthur would not have kept him a single day as lord high steward of his castle.

Both knights were of the same mind—each was eager to seize the other's fame—but their luck was not the same. It was a good, mighty joust, and Keii, however mean you may think him, splintered his spear right up to his hand. But at the same time he was lifted out of the saddle like a sack and with such force that he lay on the ground, not knowing where he was. The other then didn't want to shame him any more than just to say mockingly, "For God's sake, why are you lying there? Remember that you always made fun of those who did their best and failed. Didn't you intend to fall? If I'm not mistaken, you wanted to, for it couldn't have happened to you otherwise. You only wanted to see how it would be to fall. It's degrading in any case." When he had gotten Keii's steed, he led it to the king and said, "Sir, have one of your retinue come and take charge of this steed which I won. I don't want anything that is yours unless I gain it in another way."

The king thanked him warmly and asked, "Who are you, sir?"

"I am Iwein."

"Well, for God's sake!"

"It's no joke, sir. I am he." Then he told how he had become lord of the land. All were pleased both at the honor he had won and at Keii's disgrace, but no one as much as Sir Gawein, for he and Sir Iwein had always been close friends, and the fame they shared had now become all the greater. Sir Keii had landed hard and was still lying there, the laughingstock of them all. If a high-minded man with a sense of shame had suffered such dishonor as Keii had often met with, he would have avoided these people ever after. Keii's body pained him, but nothing else mattered, because his back was already overtaxed with a burden of disgrace. The incident couldn't make him unhappy in the least: he was used to shame. The conflict ended thus, with his mishap and with loud, scornful laughter. None of the rest could begrudge Sir Iwein his land, the spring, or all his honors. Indeed, he had so won their favor that they had no other thought than to spread his fame.

At Sir Iwein's request, the king now rode back with him to the castle. There neither want nor will kept the entertainment from being so good that King Arthur never had better except in his own country. Nothing could match that, of course, and it is also not possible that anything on earth will ever equal it. The queen was pleased and said to Sir Iwein, "Dear companion and lord, my heartfelt thanks for bringing this esteemed guest. Truly, I shall always be indebted to you." She might well be happy since,

until this moment, she had had no real proof that she was well
married. There was no doubt about it now, and for the first time,
she became truly fond of her husband. When she had the honor
of meeting the king because of him, she saw clearly that she had
been lucky, also that he had won the spring with courage and defended it as a hero. "I have chosen well," she thought.

A guest who is not a fool soon finds out how his host regards
him because, if he is unwelcome, some expression of ill humor
reveals it. When a man is staying with a friendly host, he enjoys
both food and entertainment more, but the guest is not well
cared for where there is no willingness to please: King Arthur
found both the will and the deed in the castle. Sir Gawein, who
was in every respect courtly and noble, showed his loyalty to his
friend, Sir Iwein. Wise men say that there is no stronger
force than a friendship between those who are not kin
which turns out well, for they will remain faithful to each
other even when brothers part. It was like this with Sir Gawein and his host. They were so fond of each other that each
shared the other's joy and sorrow. The well-bred Gawein
revealed his courtly manners now, and I'll tell you how.

Lunete was the name of the girl who had acted so prudently
and saved Sir Iwein from great trouble with her cleverness. Gawein sat down beside her and thanked her warmly for bringing
such honor to his friend, because it was her help that had
brought him through all sorts of danger and made him lord of
the country. Gawein said that he was grateful for her kindness.
Truly it is a good idea, when someone is glad to be helpful, to
express your thanks so that he may not tire of it, since, after all,
it takes effort. One should be angry at him who withholds his
thanks, because he perhaps will learn by it. "Lady Lunete," continued the knight, "your advice and intercession have made me
very happy, since Sir Iwein is my best friend. He told me all
about how your tact and skill brought him this honor, with
which he is justly pleased. Because of you, he has a beautiful
wife, a rich land, life itself, and whatever else one desires in this
world. If I were so respected that a woman could be honored
through me, I would devote to you my life—and I hold nothing
more dear—in payment for the crown which, due to your aid, my
comrade now wears." With this a lasting friendship between the
two was formed.

Lady Laudine and Sir Iwein received King Arthur into their
castle with such ceremony that none could help but be pleased.
After the guests had been there for seven nights, it was time for
them to depart. While they were taking leave, the faithful Sir
Gawein led Sir Iwein aside and said, "It is not surprising when a
lucky man gains much honor if he is brave and knows how to
strive for it. But many men toil day after day as best they can
and yet gain no fame: fortune simply is not with them. Your
efforts, on the other hand, have been well rewarded, for you
have won a beautiful woman and a land. Now, since things have
turned out favorably for you, take care that your wife's beauty
does not bring you shame. Friend, watch out that you do not
soon make the mistake of those who, because of their wives, are
condemned for sloth. Don't turn wholly to a life of ease, as Sir
Erec did, who was idle for a long time because of Lady Enite. If
he had not made up for it later in knightly manner, his honor
would have been lost. He was a prisoner of his love. You have all
you need to be satisfied, so let me tell you how to preserve your
fame. Come with us and we'll take part in tournaments as before. If you should lose your knightly spirit, I would be forever
sorry that I knew you.

"Many a man excuses himself, saying that it is a part of being
a householder that when one is married, one should for a time
neither ride out for knightly sport nor entertain, but only take
care of domestic duties. He gives up both social joys and stylish
clothing and calls whatever he puts on to keep warm the fashion
of the householder. He becomes peevish, goes about unkempt,
half-dressed, and barefoot, and almost the first thing he says to
a visitor is always this: 'I've had to buy grain every half year
since I first became a landowner, although no one will believe it.
And this year it is really bad. I hate to bother you with my
troubles, but the hail ruined the best field I have. I'm afraid I'll
have to give up my castle. I could get along somehow myself,
still I worry about my wife. I don't know what I would do with
her. Whoever has a household to care for has a great deal of
worry, and no one can believe how much it costs. I could meet the
demands of society in other respects if I could only manage to
support the castle.'

"So he begins to lament and tell his guest so many sad stories
that the latter wishes he had never come there. The host is right,

yet not entirely. The more it costs to run an estate, the more time its head must spend at home if he wants it to do him honor. Still, now and then he also needs to show that he has a knightly spirit by taking part in those tournaments which he should attend. I know what I am talking about. For whose sake would a good man rather be well esteemed than for that of a loyal wife? If he has given up all claim to fame, wanting to spend his time with her in indolence, and maintains—like a mean-spirited man—that he is doing it for her sake, she shouldn't accept it, since however fond of him she may be, his lack of distinction and his idleness will annoy her if he is with her too much. Through fear of their husbands, many wives pretend that they are not vexed about it, but what he gains by remaining with her in idleness he can keep for himself and no one will envy him.

"You have won a queen and a country; yet if this should now be your ruin, I think that a worthy man without an acre of land would be richer. Sir Iwein, think of this and leave with us. Be so loving that the queen will let you go away for a suitable length of time, and commend people and land to her care. As for her, a wife who has shown herself to be so steadfast needs no overseers but her own honor. Those are for faithless women and for girls who are foolish enough to be led astray even by the words of an old crone. I wouldn't want you to live otherwise than you have done: as a noble knight who is always mindful of honor. Now, more than ever, you have a right to see that your fame increases and spreads. While formerly you were hampered by having much less wealth than courage, you now have riches in keeping with your knightly spirit. Be stalwart and lighthearted, and the tournaments in many lands will be great events because of us two. Take my advice, Sir Iwein."

The knight at once sought out his wife and with success. When he presented his request, she had no thought that he would ask anything that she would not be glad to grant. However, she quickly regretted her advance assent when he asked permission to journey to tournaments. "I shouldn't have been so hasty," she said, but it was too late, and he took leave to be gone a whole year. She swore indeed that she would never forgive him if he were absent any longer. While he, impelled by his love, declared that even a year seemed too much and that he would not stay away any longer than this, in fact would return sooner

if he could, if a lawful hindrance—sickness, prison, or death—
did not prevent him. "You know very well," she replied, "that
our esteem and our land are hanging in the balance, and we
may suffer great harm if you do not return on time. Today is
the eighth day after the solstice, and that is when the year will
be up. Come then or sooner, since I shall not wait longer for
you. Let this gold ring bear witness to the compact. I have
never before loved a man enough to lend or give it to him, so
life should go all the better for him who wears it and has it to
look at. Do not lose it, Sir Iwein, because its stone has the
power to bestow good fortune and content. Who wears it is a
lucky man." King Arthur was now ready and, saying good-by,
rode away. The lady accompanied her husband some three
leagues or more; one could easily see that the parting caused
her great sorrow. Sir Iwein concealed his pain as best he could
with a smile, but his eyes were sad. Indeed, he would have
wept, were it not for his pride, and that's no lie. King Arthur
rode into his country and the lady returned to her castle.

At this point Lady Love asked me something which I am not
wise enough to answer. "Tell me, Hartmann," she said, "do you
claim that King Arthur took Sir Iwein to his castle and let his
wife just ride back?" I could defend myself only by assuring her
it was true, for it was told me as a fact. She looked at me with
mistrust and replied, "That's not so, Hartmann."

"Lady, truly I have it correct." "No," she answered. The dispute went on for some time before she put me on the right track
so that I could agree with her. Arthur had led away both man
and wife, and yet neither of them had followed him, as I shall
now explain to you. They had exchanged hearts: with the king
went the lady's heart in Sir Iwein's breast, and his heart in her
body remained behind. "My Lady Love," I spoke then, "it seems
to me that Sir Iwein is lost if he has surrendered his heart, since
it was what gave him courage and strength. How can he do
knightly deeds now? He will be as timid as a woman because he
has a woman's heart and she that of a man. She'll be the manly
one and should take part in the tournaments, while he should
stay home and take care of the castle. I am really very sorry that
their two natures have been so altered by this exchange, for neither has been helped by it."

At this Lady Love accused me of being weak-witted. "Be still," she said. "You know nothing about the best of life, for you never felt my power. I am Love and often make men and women lose their hearts and be all the stronger because of it." I didn't dare ask further questions, since I had never seen a like wonder—men and women living without hearts—anywhere, but in this case it happened as she said. All I know about their exchange is what the story tells: that Sir Iwein was without doubt a great warrior beforehand and a better one afterward.

His friend, Sir Gawein, was his downfall. I should tell you why because it is unusual for one to lose by choosing a worthy comrade. Indeed, it never happened before, but it happened to Sir Iwein, and I'll tell you how. Sir Gawein was the most courtly man who ever lived and later was sorry that his friend had to suffer on his account. He did all he could to serve Sir Iwein by increasing his fame: wherever they took part in a tournament there were exploits such as God himself might well behold. He helped him in every way—even saw to it that Sir Iwein won the prize more often than anyone else—until too many days had passed. The time went by happily for Sir Iwein. They say that Sir Gawein captivated and detained him by good entertainment so that he forgot about the deadline and his vow until far into August of the second year. They had just come gaily from a tournament, at which Sir Iwein had won the highest praise from both sides, and arrived at Karidol, where their lord, King Arthur, was having a festival. They pitched their tents on the field in front of the castle and camped there to rest until the king and the noblest of his retinue visited them with shouts of rejoicing, for the court had heard of their success. The king thanked them for having performed such feats. It is right to recognize him who likes to act honorably and it makes him happier about his efforts. Wherever people sat around talking here, they spoke only of these two.

Then Sir Iwein began to feel love's desire, and it occurred to him that he had been away from his wife a long time, indeed that he had disregarded her request and her command. His heart was seized by a painful devotion and such remorse that he forgot where he was and sat silently, like a fool, neither hearing what was said nor seeing what was going on. Bad news was drawing near of which he had forebodings, as I myself often have: sometimes when I am happy, I began to sigh over future misfortune. So it was with him as his grief approached.

Now look! There rode his wife's messenger, Lady Lunete, on whose advice he had been chosen in the first place. She hurried across the field and dismounted in front of the tents. As soon as she saw the king, she came before him and spoke: "King Arthur, my lady sent me here to your country and bade me bring her greetings to you and all your companions save one, who is not included and should be scorned by you as a traitor. He is this Sir Iwein, who, when I first saw him, didn't seem to be the kind that would be disloyal and cause pain to one to whom he had promised to be faithful. His words are noble, but his spirit is not. My lady is a woman, and it is clear, God knows, that she can't avenge herself. If there had been reprisal to fear, he would not have abused her this way. It didn't seem enough that he killed her husband, but he wanted to cause her even more sorrow and deprive her of honor and life. Sir Iwein, if my lady's youth, beauty, wealth, and many virtues mean nothing to you, why didn't you at least remember what I did for you and let her profit from the fact that I came to your aid and saved your life? It would have been all over with you if I had not intervened. I shall always be sorry that I didn't let you die: it's all my fault, even though I acted from loyalty. On my counsel she forgave the grief and distress you caused her. I praised your virtues too highly, so that at last she willing gave you herself and her land, which you were to protect. A woman can never defend herself well against a man when he acts as you have done. To be sure, we were too hasty with you, but we deserved a better reward than you gave us: it was not what you promised.

"My lady will get along all right, although what you have done is truly unjust and insulting. She is too noble and too powerful for you to treat as a common mistress, even if you were now to find out what knightly loyalty is. Loyalty means nothing to you, and you shouldn't at all please those who love loyalty and honor and understand that no one can be truly noble without loyalty. I now declare to these lords that from this time on they should consider you a traitor (and when you became one, you made me, too, unfaithful and a liar). As dear as constancy and honor are to the king, he will have reason to be forever ashamed if he keeps you here as a knight any longer. You are to stay away from my lady from now on, for she wants to get along without you. And you are to give back her ring; she sent me for it so that it wouldn't remain on an unfaithful hand." Because of his great sorrow, he just sat there and let her take the ring. She bowed to the king and left.

The scorn which Lady Lunete heaped on Sir Iwein, her abrupt departure, the blow to his honor caused by her leaving him thus with neither help nor comfort, the painful disgrace that she should question his loyalty, the great constancy of his faithful heart and its belated remorse, the loss of his land, the longing for his wife—all this robbed him of reason and every joy. In despair, his only wish was to be someplace so remote that no one would know or ever find out where he had gone. He began to hate himself, since he could blame no one else: he had been struck down by his own sword. Concerned only with himself, he stole off silently, without anyone noticing, until he was away from the tent and out of sight in the open country. His sorrow then became so great that rage and madness seized his brain. He forgot all decency, tore off his clothes until he was as bare as one's hand, and ran naked across the fields toward the wilderness.

After the maiden had ridden off, the king became sorely troubled at Sir Iwein's misfortune. He inquired where he was and asked that someone go get him since he wanted to console the knight. When he was not found, they called, but to no avail because he was far away, running toward the forest. He was a proven, fearless warrior, but as brave as he was and as steadfast in body and spirit, still Lady Love enabled a frail woman to turn both upside down, for he who had been a diamond of knightly virtue was now rushing wildly about in the forest, a fool.

Then merciful God, Who had nevertheless not entirely forsaken him, allowed him to come upon a page with a good bow and many arrows, which he seized. And when he was hungry, he did as other madmen, who can care for their stomachs even if they know nothing else. He was a fine marksman, and the forest was filled with game. He shot a great deal of what came within range of his bow, but he had to chase it down himself without the aid of hounds. He had neither kettle nor lard, neither pepper nor salt: his sauce was the pangs of hunger, which broiled and stewed the meat to make it tasty and satisfy his appetite.

When he had lived thus for a long time, he happened to come one day about noon upon a new clearing. He found there only one man, who could readily see that he was not in his right mind and fled into the nearby hut to save himself. The man still did not feel safe, so he firmly barred the door in front of which stood the madman, who seemed to him like a giant. "If he gives it one push," the hermit thought, "the door will come off its hinges, and it will be all over with me. Poor me, how shall I save myself?" At last he thought of something: "Maybe he will let me live if I give him some of my bread." He stretched his hand through a window in the wall and laid a loaf of bread down on the sill. Hunger made it taste good even though, God knows, the madman had never before eaten anything so wretched. But what do you expect of one in this state? He ate the bread, drank some water he found in a pail hanging on the wall, and quickly left.

The hermit watched him go and urgently prayed that God would forevermore spare him such guests, for he knew nothing about the intruder. The latter soon showed that children and fools adapt themselves easily. He was sane enough to return in two days for something to eat, carrying on his back a deer, which he threw down in front of the door. This caused the hermit to pass out his bread and water more willingly. He was no longer afraid, became friendlier, and always had food and drink ready. The other paid him for his trouble with game. This was roasted over a fire just as it was, since the hermit had no pepper, salt, or vinegar. At last he began to sell the skins and buy for both of them enough of what they needed most: salt and better bread.

Living on this food, the noble madman remained thus in the forest until his body was like that of a Moor and no one would have guessed to look at him that he had ever enjoyed the favor of a highborn lady, struck fire from a helmet, broken a hundred spears in a day, bravely won great fame, been clever and courtly, noble and rich. For now he ran about bare of clothing and reason and did so until one noon when three ladies happened to find him sleeping near the highway along which they were riding. As soon as one of them caught sight of him, she

came, bent over him, and looked at him carefully. Everyone was
talking about Iwein's disappearance—it was a widespread tale
throughout the country—and it was partly for this reason that
she recognized him, but also because she noticed a scar that had
been well known for a long time. She spoke his name and,
looking back toward the others, said, "My lady, if Sir Iwein is
alive, then this is he lying here, or else I've never seen him." Her
tenderness and kindness troubled her heart, and—from great
sorrow and pure sympathy—she began to weep bitterly that so
fine a man should suffer the disgrace of being seen in this
shameful state.

She spoke again to the one who was mistress of the other two:
"My lady, you can easily tell that he has lost his mind, for there
was never a more courtly knight than Sir Iwein, whom I see here
in such a miserable condition. And I am as sure of this as of
death, my lady: if we heal him, you will be freed from all the distress which Count Aliers in his arrogance has long caused you
and still has in mind for you. I know well how brave Sir Iwein is.
If he recovers, he will quickly defeat your enemy. If you are to be
saved, it must be through his help."

The lady was happy at this good news. "If the sickness comes
from the brain," she said, "I can easily help him because I still
have a salve which Feimorgan made with her own hands. Its
power is such that anyone who suffers from a brain ailment will
at once regain health and strength when treated with it." So
they agreed to try and all three rode on in haste to get the
ointment, for their castle was hardly a league away: the young
lady was sent back within an hour and found him still asleep.
On giving her the box of salve, her mistress strictly ordered her
not to spread it all over him, only where he was ailing, since the
sickness would then pass away and he would at once recover.
She was to rub on just enough and bring back the rest because
many people could be healed with it. Her mistress also sent
fresh clothing with her: one article of fine linen, another of red
wool, wool trousers, and shoes. She rode to where he was
sleeping in the forest and led a very gentle horse—with a splendid bridle and gold-trimmed saddle and saddlecloth—so that he
might ride if God allowed her to heal him.

Seeing him lying there as before, she didn't delay, but tied the
two horses fast to a limb, went up to him so quietly that he was

not aware of her, and—without saying a word—smeared the precious salve over him from head to foot. She felt such pity for him that she continued until the box was empty, which was quite needless and, moreover, had been forbidden. However, her good will would not have thought it enough if she had had six times as much, she was so eager to see him healed. Knowing that the pain of nakedness is painful to a decent man, she quickly left him as soon as the salve was gone and tactfully hid where she could watch him but he could not see her. "If he comes to his senses," she thought, "and discovers that I have seen him naked, it will be bad for me because he will never want to look me in the face." She therefore did not show herself until the salve had taken effect and he had become sane.

When he sat up, looked at himself, and saw how dreadful he appeared, he said, "Is it you, Iwein, or someone else? Have I been sleeping till now? Oh, Lord! If so, let me sleep on forever! For my dream gave me a splendid life. Oh, what esteem was mine while I slept! I dreamed such great things for myself. I was young and highborn, rich and handsome (not at all like this), well mannered and clever, and (if my dream did not deceive me) had gained much hard-won fame with knightly deeds. I got what I wanted with spear and sword. My strong arm won me a rich land and a wife, with whom I spent little time (so I dreamed) before King Arthur led me away from her to his castle; in my dream it seemed that my comrade was Sir Gawein. She gave me leave to be gone a year (but none of this is really true) and I needlessly stayed away longer, until, to my dismay, she withdrew her affection. In the midst of these fantasies I awoke. My dream made me a powerful lord (I would have been glad to die while enjoying those honors) but it was mocking me. Who gives heed to dreams comes to shame.

"Dream, how strange you are! In a moment you give wealth and power to a wretched man who never even hoped to gain esteem, but when he wakes up, you make him a fool like me. Yet, as unkempt a peasant as I am, if I were at knightly games with a steed and arms, I am sure I could do as well as those who were always noblemen." He was confused and a stranger to himself: it seemed to him that he had only dreamed his life and journeys as a knight. "My dream taught me something," he said, "and I shall win fame if I can get an outfit. It took away the traits of my

class, for although I am a peasant, my mind is full of jousting.
My heart is not at all like my body: the one is rich and the other
is poor. Did I really dream all that? If not, who made me look so
ugly? But I must indeed give up this knightly turn of mind since
I lack both the figure and the wealth to go with it." Then he saw
with surprise the new clothing lying beside him and said,
"These are clothes like the many I wore in my dream, and since I
don't see anyone here to whom they belong, they shall be mine,
for I surely need them. I wonder if they will become me as well.
Before, in my dream, fine clothing looked so splendid on me." He
dressed at once and, as soon as his black body was covered,
looked just like a knight.

When the young lady saw that he was sitting there decently
clad, she mounted her horse and slyly rode toward him, leading
the second horse. She neither looked his way nor spoke, but
acted as if merely intending to ride past. Seeing her about to go
by, he would have sprung to his feet if he had not been so
weakened by sickness that he couldn't get up as quickly as he
wanted. He therefore called to her, but she pretended to be in a
hurry and unaware of his presence until he called a second time.
Then she turned and answered saying, "Who's calling me?"
"Come this way, lady," he replied. "All right, sir," she said and
rode up to stop in front of him. She spoke, "I am at your service
and shall be glad to do what you request," and then asked how
he had come there. "I just found myself here sick," answered Sir
Iwein—he surely looked it—"and can't tell you what wondrous
event brought me to this place, but I can assure you that I don't
want to stay. You will do me a great kindness if you take me
with you, and I shall forever seek to repay you suitably." "I'll do
that, knight," she said, "and for your sake shall interrupt the
journey on which my lady, the ruler of this land, sent me. I'll
take you to her and I would indeed advise you to rest up after all
the troubles you've had."

So he mounted the horse, and she took him to her lady, who
had never been happier to see a man. He was well cared
for—with clothing, food, a bath—until he showed no effects of
his illness. Sir Iwein found good treatment here and recovered
from his distress. The lady did not forget to ask about her salve,
but the clever girl talked herself out of the difficulty with a story

she made up. "I am very sorry to tell you, lady," she said, "what happened to me and the box. It is a wonder that I am alive because I almost drowned—the knight saw it happen. I had a narrow escape when I rode over the river on the high bridge nearby. Damn the horse! It stumbled and fell clear to its knees so that I lost the rein and could hardly stay in the saddle. I forgot about the box and it fell into the water. Believe me, no loss ever caused me such distress. What good does it do to be careful? One will surely lose whatever one is not destined to keep." As plausible as this lie was, her mistress was still pretty angry. "We've had good luck and bad," she declared, "I can say that indeed. But we'll have to make the best of the loss and thank God for what we've gained. In a short time I've found a knight and lost my precious ointment. Well, because of what I've won, I'll forget about the harm done. It's useless to grieve over lost goods which can't be regained." With this her wrath was gone.

Sir Iwein therefore stayed here until the wild appearance left him and he became a handsome man, as before. They at once got him the best armor that could be found and the finest steed in the land. So the guest was well equipped and lacked nothing.

One morning Count Aliers was seen approaching with his army, and led by Sir Iwein, the knights of the country and their squires prepared to attack. Formerly they had been so hard pressed by mounted companies that they had almost lost courage and had stayed behind firmly barred gates without trying to defend the land. But their spirits rose when they saw their guest charge the enemy so bravely. Those who had been despondent now looked at him and took heart.

Sir Iwein let the lady see from the battlements that a good deed done an honest man is often repaid. She did not regret anything she had given him, since his courage alone caused the enemy to retreat in disorder to a ford. They recovered there, and a great battle began. Who could tell of all the spears which Sir Iwein broke? He and his men fought so fiercely that the others fled in confusion from the ford with many losses, granting them the victory. Of those who didn't flee, most were killed at once; the rest were taken captive. The conflict turned out to the hero's honor as everyone began to praise him, saying that he was brave, courtly, and wise, and that nothing could harm them if they had

him or someone like him for their lord. It was their fervent wish
that he and their lady would find it suitable to marry.

So it was that those in Count Aliers's army were quickly and
boldly captured or slain. Yet he and a small company fought on
and performed valiant deeds that no one could belittle. When it
was hopeless to continue, he, too, had to retreat, and he fled,
fighting as he went, toward one of his fortresses which was nearby. But the mountain on which it stood was so high and the
castle road so steep and long that, in spite of all he could do, he
was overtaken at the gate by Sir Iwein. The latter captured him
and made him swear to ride back as a prisoner and be subject to
the power of the lady who had often suffered because of him,
whose lands he had laid waste. (He later gave her security and
hostages to guarantee that he would make good all the damage
to her full satisfaction.)

No knight was ever honored more than was Sir Iwein when
they saw him riding up with his prisoner by his side. When the
countess received him and went to him, accompanied by all her
ladies, one could catch sight of many loving glances. She kept
looking at him and would have given him any reward he asked
for, holding back neither her possessions nor herself. But he was
not so inclined and wanted no reward at all. Now that he had
freed the lady of Narison from distress, he asked leave to go. She
didn't want to grant it because she was in love with him and
thought he would make a fine lord for the land. If it had not
seemed too brazen, she would have offered him her hand.
However, if I'm not mistaken, it would have been wiser for her to
woo someone who would not cause her any harm—although no
one does it—than to let herself be courted by a man who would
bring her misfortune. Her manner spoke plainly enough, but he
paid no attention. Both the words and the fond glances which
tried to keep him there were wasted, for he said good-by and,
taking the first road he found, rode off at once.

He was following the highway when he heard a voice that was
very loud and terrible, but also plaintive. It led him into the forest, through a great tangle of fallen trees, and to a clearing in
which a fierce battle was raging: a dragon and a lion were
fighting savagely. The dragon was large and powerful, and from
its jaws shot forth a stream of fire. It was the heat and stench of

this which caused the lion to roar so loudly. For a moment Sir
Iwein was troubled by doubt about which he should help but decided to aid the noble beast, even though he was afraid that
would not keep it from attacking him as soon as the dragon was
dead. For the way things are—and this is also true of people—when one has served a stranger as well as possible, one
should still be careful not to be duped. Such was the case here,
but as a brave man, he took the chance. Dismounting, he
charged at the dragon, struck it dead, and thus helped the lion in
its need. After he had slain its enemy, he half expected the beast
to attack him, but he soon learned otherwise when the lion lay
down at his feet and, with voice and manner, gave him a word-
less greeting. It stopped its fearful raging and showed him affection as well as a beast could. It became his follower and from
then on served him faithfully in many ways, going wherever he
went and standing by him in every danger until death parted
them.

They had not gone far when the lion scented prey, which
hunger as well as its nature made it want to hunt down at once.
It could tell this to Sir Iwein only by halting, looking at him, and
pointing with its head, but it let him know thus. He urged it on
like a hound and, leaving the road, followed for a stone's throw.
The lion found a deer standing there and, quickly catching it,
began to suck the warm blood. Its master didn't care for blood;
however, he stripped off the hide where he knew the best and
fattest meat to be and cut off a large piece. Since night was then
falling, he made a fire and, roasting his meal, ate it unsalted and
without bread and wine. Nothing finer was to be had. The lion
devoured all the rest but the bones. Afterward Sir Iwein lay
down and slept while the lion circled around him and his horse,
keeping watch. It intended to guard him faithfully at all times
and did so, both then and later. These were their tasks for two
weeks: the man rode about seeking *aventiure* while the wild lion
provided him with such game as food.

At last fate quite unexpectedly led him straight to his lady's
country, where he found the same spring which—as I have
already told you—brought him both great happiness and bitter
sorrow. When he saw the linden above it and when the chapel
and the stone appeared before him, his heart was reminded of

how he had lost honor, land, and wife. He became so sad and tor-
mented by grief that he almost lost his mind again, and his
heart so failed him that he fell from his horse, pale as death. As
he was bending far over forward, his sword sprang from its
sheath and was sharp enough to cut through his hauberk and
give him a great wound that bled severely. This troubled the
lion, which thought him dead and wanted to die, too. It leaned
the sword against a bush and would have leapt on it to drive the
blade into its belly if Sir Iwein had not shown signs of life. However, he sat up and thus kept the lion from killing itself.

Lamenting his misfortune, the knight said, "Unlucky man,
what is your lot now? You are the most wretched person ever
born. How could you so lose the affection of your lady! If anyone
else in the world were guilty of this, it would cost him his life. A
man who never won honors is happier than one who did but was
not wise enough to keep them. I had such fame and happiness
that I lament to God that I gained so much, since it was not to
last. If I hadn't had a great deal of good fortune and pleasure, I
wouldn't know what it was like and would have lived on, un-
troubled and without pangs of longing, as before. But desire tor-
ments me now that I must look at my loss and shame in my
lady's land. This is her country and heritage. It was once in my
hands so that I could have whatever I wished, and now I have no
claim at all to it. I have also good cause to lament the loss of my
lovely wife. Why do I spare my life? If my own sword were to
avenge me on myself and run me through, it would be no more
than I deserve. Since I have done this to myself—since it was my
own misdeed and no fault of hers that caused me quite needlessly to lose the affection of my lady and to exchange laughter
for tears—I should be punished for it. This wild lion who wanted
to kill himself because of grief for me has shown me that true
loyalty is no small thing.'

This bitter complaint was heard by a girl who was suffering
more from fear than any woman before her, for she was lying in
the chapel, a prisoner and condemned to death. She had been
looking out through a crack in the door as Sir Iwein spoke and
now she said, "Who is lamenting there?" "Who is it that asks?"
he replied. "Sir," she answered, "she who is grieving in here is a
girl who is more wretched than any other alive, no matter what

her plight or how great her sorrow." "Who could cause you such distress as I suffer?" he asked. "You have no reason to complain. I am the one who is really cursed." "It isn't possible for your trouble to be as great as mine," she replied. "I can see that you are able to stand and walk and ride wherever you wish while I am a prisoner and tomorrow shall be hanged or burned, for there is no one to save my life." "How did that happen, lady?" he asked. "May I never win God's grace if I am at all guilty," she said, "but I am imprisoned here as a traitor. My countrymen have charged me with so grave a crime that I would indeed deserve severe punishment if I were not innocent. Last year the mistress of the land entered into a marriage which unfortunately did not turn out well, and I was blamed. My God, how could I help it that she made a mistake with him? That I ever advised her to marry him was truly for the sake of her honor, and I still cannot understand how such a fine man can behave so badly. He was really the best one I've ever known. However, my present state is just my misfortune and not his fault. Well, this is why I am struggling with despair. They have given me until tomorrow and then shall take my life because, sad to say, I am only a woman and cannot defend myself through combat, and there is no one else to save me."

"I must admit that your plight is more fearful than mine," said Sir Iwein, "since you will die unless you find some means of defense." "Who could save me?" she asked. "Even if someone wanted to, he wouldn't have the strength to avoid defeat, for there are three strong men accusing me. I know only two knights who are so mighty and brave, and who would undertake such a difficult task for poor me. Either of them could slay a whole army of people like these without even a weapon. And I am as sure of this as of death: if either knew of my distress, he would come and fight for me. But I can't reach them in time and therefore must die, because I can't expect help from anyone else." "Name me the three men who challenge you," said the knight, "and also the two who are brave enough to fight alone against three." "I'll tell you who they all are," she answered. "The three in whose power I am are the lord high steward and his brothers. They have always envied and hated me because my lady thought better of me than they liked, and now they have won her over so that she doesn't care what happens to me. After this husband—who had appeared well suited to my lady—forsook her, they never ceased to make trouble for me every day. They accused me of disloyalty, saying that it was my guile alone that caused things to go so badly for her. Whatever happens to me, I won't deny that my advice led her to marry him: judging by his past, I was sure he would be a help to her and bring her honor. But now they lie about me, saying that I betrayed her. When they began to abuse me, I was greatly distressed and, alone and forsaken, became rash with anger. Who can't control his resentment and speaks too hastily ruins his chances, and unfortunately that's what I did. I brought about my own destruction.

"Because I was angry, I said that if the three bravest men at the court dared to make charges against me, I would find in forty days a knight who would fight them all at once. I was too rash: they accepted the challenge and wouldn't let me withdraw it. Moreover, I had to take an oath that I would carry out my offer just as I had made it and would prove my innocence by combat in six weeks. I rode away to look for the two in whom I had placed my hopes but found neither of them. Then I went to King Arthur's court. However, I couldn't find anyone there who would help me and left without a champion. Because of this I suffered such ridicule on my return that it almost broke my heart. Then they locked me in here, and I am now just waiting to die, for those who could save me are far away. Both would help me in my great need if they knew of it, either Sir Gawein or Sir Iwein."

"Which Iwein do you mean?" asked the knight. "Sir," she replied, "it is the one who brought on my imprisonment, the son of King Urien. He is the cause of the trouble I am in. I was too eager to gain his favor and worked too hard to make him lord here, which—sad to say—he became. I shouldn't have been won to him so quickly: it takes a long time to get to know someone. Thinking he would reward me much better than he did, I was overhasty in praising him, and it was on my advice that my lady gave herself and her land to him. Now he has deceived us both and harmed himself as well. It is his misfortune, too, because my mistress is so noble, beautiful, and rich. I would swear that he will never in the world make a better marriage. Even if she were only his equal, he should be glad to have her accept him."

"Are you Lunete?" asked the knight. "I am, sir," she replied. "Then learn who I am," he said, "that wretched Iwein. May God pity me for ever being born! How could I have lost my lady's affection! But since the fault is mine—I don't know whom else to blame—the injury, too, should be mine. My greatest burden now is life itself, but i'll soon be rid of it. I am sure I can defeat all three knights who locked you in there, and when I have set you free, I'll kill myself. My lady shall see the combat because she must be present when it takes place. I don't know anything better to do than to give her justice by condemning myself tomorrow morning and dying for her sake before her eyes, since death will surely end my pain and longing. This shall happen without her knowing who I am until I and the three on whom I shall avenge you are dead. When my lady finds out that it is I, she will know that I lost my life because of grief. She shall see herself avenged.

"It is right that I should repay you for the noble crown which I wore because of your aid. I had many honors, but what good did it do me to find gold? The finding of gold doesn't help a fool: he just throws it away at once. However, whatever I have done to myself, you may be sure that I shall not forsake you, for you rescued me when I would otherwise have been killed. Tomorrow I shall do the same for you." Then he took off his helmet, and she could see that it really was Sir Iwein. She was no longer distressed and, weeping with joy, said what she thought: "Now that I have seen my lord alive, nothing can harm me. I was afraid that you had been slain. At court I heard no news about where you might be."

"Lady Lunete," answered Sir Iwein, "where was the knight who has always done whatever is requested by the ladies who seek his aid, my dear friend, Sir Gawein, who has always striven to please them? If you had told him what you wanted, he would have done everything you asked." "If I had

found him," she replied, "my worries would have been over
at once. That I didn't find him was due to a strange event.
The queen had been abducted from Arthur's court by a
knight, and everyone was eager to defeat and shame him.
Sir Gawein had ridden after him and was absent when I
arrived with my complaint. Truly, I left them lamenting
both the lady and Sir Gawein's pursuit, since they were
afraid that they had lost her forever and that he would lose
his life, for he didn't intend to return without finding out
where she had been taken."

The story made Sir Iwein concerned about his friend.
"May God protect him," he said, "but now, lady, I must
leave you and get ready. Expect me tomorrow morning: I'll
be on time for the combat. And please tell no one who I am.
I shall indeed help you in your distress and defeat all three
of them or die." "Dear sir," she answered, "it would be a
mistake to risk so worthy a life for such a poor woman; this
is too much for me to ask. I'll accept the intent in place of
the deed and release you from your promise, for your life is
of more use than mine. If it could be an equal fight, I would
venture to ask for your help, but no one is ever expected to
fight three men. People claim that even two are too many, so
this would be no contest at all. If you were to lose your life
because of me, I would be the most unhappy woman who
ever lived, and then they would kill me also. It is better for
me to perish alone than for us both to die." "The affair will
turn out better than that," he said, "for they won't kill either
of us. I want to comfort you since I shall make my words
come true. You have done so much for me that—if I have
any loyalty at all—I can't see you harmed when I can
prevent it. But enough of this; they shall let you go or I'll
slay all three of them." Her honesty caused her to regret
that which served her own need and esteem: she wanted to
be saved, yet not at the cost of his life. However, as he chose
the combat without being urged, she agreed to it. Indeed, she
could not have stopped him.

Sir Iwein remained no longer, but rode on—his lion behind
him as always—until he saw a castle, the home of a noble
knight. It was strongly fortified, and well protected in every

way from assault and catapults by a high, thick wall that enclosed the hill on which it stood. Still, the lord of the castle had a distressing view before him because his town had been burned down right up to the wall. Sir Iwein came riding along, following the road, and then turned off toward the castle. The drawbridge was let down and he saw approach him six handsome squires who, in figure and dress, would have done honor to the emperor. They gave him a friendly welcome. Soon afterward their lord, a courteous man, came, greeted him, and led him into a fine hall where there was a splendid company of knights and ladies. Sir Iwein took note of their behavior and disposition and found both pleasing.

Who has gone through great troubles has much more sympathy with another's need than one who has never known distress. The lord of the castle had been himself a knight errant who had often risked his life in combat and was therefore the better disposed toward his guest. He sat beside Sir Iwein all the time the servants were removing his armor, and the entire company showed its good will, doing him more honor than was needful. For their guest's sake, they acted joyful, although their hearts were not in it. A bitter grief, of which Sir Iwein as well as other strangers knew nothing, daily banished their happiness so that their gaiety was quite hollow. Forced merriment, which has the lips laughing while the heart breaks with sorrow, is worthless and also not hard to see through: a sensible man will know that which does not come from the heart. In any case, they could not keep up the pretense, and their worry and fear of the next day conquered their gaiety. Sorrow won the contest, and in less time than it takes to tell, their joyful appearance turned to weeping and wailing. When Sir Iwein saw this, he asked his host what had happened.

"For God's sake tell me, sir," he said. "What is the trouble and what does this sudden change mean? Why have you and your people, just now so happy, altered so?" To this the lord of the castle replied, "It would be better for you not to ask about the calamity which oppresses us. However, if you insist, I'll tell you, although I would be sorry to make you sad.

It would be best to hear nothing about it so that you can be
happy with those who are fortunate. I am Misfortune's child
and must grieve with the unlucky ones: that is my lot.

His guest then did insist until he revealed all his sorrow.
"My life is forever hateful to me," he said, "because I grow
old in disgrace. I would be better off dead, for I am suffering
shame and distress from a man so powerful that I cannot
avenge myself. A giant named Harpin has robbed me of
everything except this castle and has turned my estate into
a wasteland. And I'll tell you how little I am to blame. I
have a daughter, a beautiful girl, and he is destroying my
possessions because I refused to give her to him. Truly, I
would rather lose my property and risk my life than see her
his wife. I have also six sons who are knights. He captured
them and hanged two before my eyes—who has ever suffered
worse? He still has four, and I shall soon lose them, too. Tomorrow he is going to bring them up to the castle and kill
them right in front of me if I do not give him their sister.
May God let me die tonight so that I won't have to endure
that! What pains me the worst is that he says he won't take
her as his wife when he gets her by this villainy, but will
give her to the meanest servant he has. Why shouldn't my
life be a burden? If I have deserved this shameful offense
because of my sins, I wish God would punish only me and
not vent His wrath on my innocent children, who are upright and good."

Sir Iwein's heart was moved at seeing and hearing of the
lord's grief. "Why haven't you sought help where it can be
had," he asked, "in King Arthur's land? You didn't need to
endure this outrage so long. You would have found someone
among his companions who would have freed you of the
giant." "He who would have been the most help," replied his
host, "and would have come if he had known or if I had
found him is out of the country now. The king also has suffered an offense of which he would like to be free. I'll tell
you a strange story if you want to hear it. A week ago a
knight came there, just when he knew those of the Round
Table would be sitting with the king. He dismounted in front
of them and said, 'I have come with a request. Lord, I have

heard of your generosity and nobility and feel sure that the gift I ask of you and for which I came will not be denied.' To this King Arthur replied, 'Any petition which you present here will be granted if it is proper.' 'You should leave that to me,' was the answer. 'It is not in keeping with your fame for you to make reservations. You honor me by leaving me free to ask what I will, whatever it may be. Otherwise I shall forgo the request.'

"King Arthur declined, and the knight left his court in a rage. 'A lot of people have been deceived about this king,' he said, 'and the whole world has spread lies concerning him. Of his generosity it has been said that no knight was ever denied what he asked. Whoever thinks well of him has a fickle sense of honor.' All the knights of the Round Table heard his loud scolding and spoke with one voice, 'Sir, it would be wrong for you to let the knight go away like this. Whom have you ever refused anything? Trust his decency; he looks like a man who would make reasonable requests. If he leaves in such anger, he will never again speak well of you.'

"The king thought it over, had someone bring him back, and promised him whatever he asked. The knight needed no further pledge since the king's word was as good as a formal oath. The arrogant fellow then asked to be allowed to take away the queen, his wife. The king was stunned. 'I've been tricked,' he cried, 'and betrayed by those who advised me!' When the knight saw how angry he was, he consoled him, saying, 'Sir, remember your good manners and consider that I ask for her only on the condition that I can get her out of the country, defeating all those who pursue me to rescue her, even though you have an army of the best of knights. I won't hurry any more than usual, and whoever chases me may know that I won't ride a bit faster because of him and will turn to meet him.'

"The king then had to keep his promise, and the knight led the queen away. She looked at all of them pitiably when she left, as one fearing greatly for her honor, and begged them urgently with words and demeanor to free her quickly. The court was never so troubled before or since, but those who saw her go were not cowed. There was a great commotion: from everywhere came the call, 'Bring my steed and armor!' and each set out in pursuit as soon as he could get ready. 'Since he has agreed to this,' they said, 'things will turn out all right. Unless God Himself is on his side, he won't take her far.' 'If neither God nor the devil protects him who so insulted us by this great offense to my lady,' spoke up Sir Keii, 'he will be put to shame. I am lord high steward here, and I surely owe it to King Arthur to free my lady, his wife, with a will. Truly, it will cost that man his life: he won't take her the length of a field without my leave. By God, if he had known I was here, he would never have come to the court with such a request. I'll soon get her back. You should be ashamed to go chasing after him all together. What good is this senseless uproar, and why should the whole court ride out after one man? I can easily defeat him alone. He won't even try to defend himself when he sees that it is I: what good would it do him? You can all stay here since I've taken this on. I'll save you the trouble.'

"By now he was ready and was the first to overtake the knight, also the first to be defeated. They were in a forest when he ordered the stranger to turn. The latter did so at once and knocked Sir Keii out of the saddle with great force, so that his helmet caught in a branch and he remained hanging by the neck. If his friend the devil had not saved him, he surely would have died, but as it was, he suffered a lot of pain. He was later freed, sad to say; however, he hung there long enough for all to see his shame and distress. The next to come was Kalogrenant, who found him hanging from the tree like a thief and didn't get him down; he was pleased at the sight. He, too, charged at the stranger and just missed the same fate when he also was unhorsed.

"Haste, ill will, and Keii's spiteful nature caused those who later saw him hanging there to ride on. The fierce Dodines caught up with the stranger in a clearing and broke a spear on him, but was himself thrown onto the grass a good spear's length behind his steed. Segremors overtook him then, with like success, and it was no different with Henete, who followed. Pliopleherin and Millemargot, to their

great chagrin, had similar mishaps, as did their friend Iders.
There is no need to name each knight I know, since all those
who pursued the stranger were strewn along the way, one
after the other. He encountered nobody who could free the
lady. Sir Gawein, always the paragon of knighthood, would
have come to her aid, but unfortunately he was away at the
time. He arrived the next morning and, on hearing the
king's lament, hurried after the stranger, determined to get
back the queen or die. It was then that I came looking for
him—as I must lament to God—and did not find him there.
His connection to me is such that he would have to stand by
me in my need: my wife is his sister. I just got back yesterday, without hope since I returned without him. I have good
cause to grieve because tomorrow I shall be fully disgraced."

The knight with the lion felt very sorry for him and said,
"At noon tomorrow I must be at a certain place, on the
entreaty of a lady to whom I am greatly indebted and who
will lose her life if I am late. However, if you are sure that
the giant will come to us early enough for me to do my
duty—conquer him or die—and still get to the spot by mid-
day where I have promised to be, then I'll fight him for you
and your noble wife, because her brother is as dear to me as
myself." The lord's wife and daughter now appeared. Sir
Iwein had never seen a young girl more beautiful than the
latter would have been if she had not worn herself out so
with weeping. The two gave him a friendly greeting, as one
does a beloved guest.

"It would be well for you to pay your respects to our
guest," said his host, "for he took on our trouble at once and,
God willing, is going to save us; he says he will fight our
enemy. When I told him my sad story, he promised, without
my asking, that he would defeat the giant who has caused
me so much distress or die. It is my wish and command that
you kneel before him in thanks." "God forbid that I should
ever see the sister of Sir Gawein at my feet," spoke up Sir
Iwein. "That would be too much even if it were King Arthur.
I'll be forever indebted to her if she will spare me, unworthy
as I am, such a great honor, because simple thanks is
enough for me. I'll tell you under what condition I will fight

him. As I just promised, if he appears early enough so that
after the battle I can at noon come to the aid of her who already has my word, I'll oppose him: for your sake, to please
my lady here, and because you are innocent of any wrong
doing."

They were happy at this and arranged pleasant amuse-
ments for him. Indeed, they couldn't do too much to show
their high esteem and thought it only his due. They were
loud in his praise: he seemed to them noble, honest, and
knightly in every respect. Everyone observed that the lion
was always near him and acted no different than a sheep.
Sir Iwein had a fine meal and a good night's sleep here.
Awakening at daybreak, he heard an early mass and prepared to fight him who was to come. When no one appeared,
he was concerned and said, "Sir, I am ready and willing to
serve you, but where is he? This waiting doesn't suit me at
all: I am delaying much too long. Every moment I tarry here
is a further risk to my honor. It is time for me to go."

They were frightened by the threat of his leaving and became as sad as before. Their greatest worry was to know
how to honor him most and thus change his mind. But when
the lord offered him his estate, Sir Iwein replied, "It is not
my purpose to risk my life to gain wealth," and refused it.
Then his host, the lady, the girl, and the entire retinue became pale with anxiety. In their entreaties the wife and
daughter often implored him to help them for the sake of his
best friend, Sir Gawein, and also urgently reminded him
that our Lord God grants His favor and man's esteem to the
merciful, that God would reward him for aiding them. He
was noble and kind and was deeply moved by this. It is said
that he was greatly distressed by their earnest pleas—when
he clearly saw their great need—and by their speaking so
often of God and Sir Gawein, either of whom he would have
been most glad to serve.

He was therefore troubled by doubts and thought, "I really
need wisdom to decide what would be better, because the game
I am playing has suddenly become involved, and no more or
less than all my honor is at stake. I could surely use some
good advice, for I know I shall lose whatever I do. I cannot

do both nor neglect both, nor even one of the tasks. If I
could, I wouldn't be worried, but as things are, I am simply
at a loss. I'll be dishonored if I go and disgraced if I stay. I
can't fight both battles and dare not give up either. May
God, Who has led me thus far, help me make the right
choice. I truly don't want to forsake her whom I first
promised aid, who is frightened and in danger only because
of me. How could an honest man do that? But if I hadn't
given my word, it would be easier to console myself about
her death than about the misfortune which would happen
here. For this lord, who likewise wants my help, is surely
worthy of it, as are also Sir Gawein's sister and her daughter, who move my heart for their own sakes as well as for
the sake of him to whom I owe so much that I should not refuse him any service. If I have to leave them, they will always think me a coward."

Sir Iwein's doubts and lamenting ended with the appearance of the huge giant for whom they were waiting, who now
came riding up to the castle, leading his prisoners. He had
treated them in a vile manner. Their arms, legs, and feet
were bare; indeed, they had no clothing except for the most
wretched shirts ever worn by a kitchen boy (of coarse, black,
and torn sackcloth). They were driven along by a dwarf who
had beaten them with his whip until they were covered with
blood. Sir Iwein was moved to pity by their great distress.
Their hands were bound tightly behind their backs with
bast, and their feet were tied together under the bellies of
horses that were hardly more than skin and bones and
limped and stumbled from weakness. The tails of these nags
were woven together so that they were firmly linked in
pairs. The sons looked so pitiful that I am surprised the
heart of the noble father did not break with grief when he
saw them. It was truly a woeful sight. The giant led them
thus up to the castle gate and shouted that he would hang
all four unless their sister was given over at once as a
ransom.

Then the hope of those within, the knight with the lion,
spoke to his host, "Sir, I shall indeed free our friends if I can.
God will strike down this brute. Both his monstrous in-

solence and the fact that you are in the right give me
strength. He isn't even ashamed of this outrage. He ought to
respect their noble birth and name, whatever they might
have done to him. It ill befits me to censure any knight but
still he shall pay for his crudeness. Truly, I'll make him suffer for it if I can." It took very little time for him to tie on
his helmet and get ready for combat; he had learned this
from much practice. His horse was brought, and he ordered
that the drawbridge be lowered. Then he said, "This will end
in pain and disgrace for one or even both of us. I believe my
hands will humble his threats, but in any case, I shall free
your sons or die in the attempt. We shall see right now what
happens." With this he charged at the giant, his lion close
behind him.

When the giant saw him coming, he jeered at him, saying,
"Oh, you fool! What has come over you that you are so eager
to die? It is stupid. The one who advised you to do this
doesn't want you to live and only wants to get a terrible
revenge for some harm you have caused him. He has
succeeded well, for I'll soon take care that you never again
do him either good or evil." To this Sir Iwein answered,
"Knight, why bother with threats? I'd be more likely to fear
a dwarf than you, for all your size, if all you are going to do
is shout abuse. Leave the scolding to ill-bred women who
can't fight. If our Lord supports the right, you'll soon fall."

The giant's strength and courage had taught him who
could and who could not harm him and which weapon suited
him best, and he thought himself armed well enough with
the staff he carried. Pleased that his foe had no other weapon, Sir Iwein resolutely clapped his spear under his arm,
spurred his horse, took aim at the giant's breast, and struck
him so hard that the spearhead broke off and remained
lodged in his body. For his part, the giant hit Sir Iwein a
mighty blow. I assure you that he would have been killed if
a second had landed, but his horse dashed forward with him
until he was able to draw his sword. Sir Iwein then quickly
turned and rode at his foe again, and through skill, strength,
and courage, managed to give him another wound. However,
while the horse was bearing him away, the giant struck him

such a blow that he fell forward on its neck as if dead. The
lion saw the danger he was in, rushed fiercely at the huge
man, and tore open clothing and flesh the length of his back,
from the shoulders down. Roaring like a bull, the monstrous
fellow swung his pole around, but it leaped back as he
struck. He thus missed both the lion and the chance to finish
off Sir Iwein. He struck so hard that he bent forward with
the blow and almost fell. Before he could swing again, Sir
Iwein got revenge by slashing him deeply twice and then
thrusting the sword through his heart. He crashed to the
ground like a tree, and the battle was over.

There was great rejoicing among all those who benefitted
by the giant's defeat. The knight with the lion brought them
good fortune, and after the death of their enemy, they lived
without fear or distress for the rest of their lives. They were
indeed grateful to the one who had slain him. Sir Iwein said
goodbye at once since he dared not delay any longer if he
was to preserve his honor with her who was imprisoned because of him, to whose aid he was supposed to come at mid-
day. His host begged him urgently to get some rest, but he
might as well have kept silent, for Sir Iwein could not and
dared not. The knight and his wife placed both their possessions and themselves at his disposal and thanked him in
every way they could. Their guest then said, "If I have been of
service and you want to repay me, do this one thing, and I
shall be well rewarded. I am very fond of Sir Gawein, as he
is—I well know—of me. There was never true friendship if
ours is not, which I want to show him whenever I can. Sir,
ride to him with a greeting from me. Take along your sons
who were set free, their sister, and the dwarf whose master lies here slain, and thank him for the service I rendered
you, since I did it for his sake. If he asks who I am, say that
there is a lion with me and that he will know me by it when
we meet."

The lord promised to do this and urged him to come back
after the combat at the fountain, adding that he would sup-
ply him with every comfort. "I'm not sure I can return,"
answered Sir Iwein. "I would like to if those I must fight let
me. However, I don't expect they will allow me to ride away

at all if they can prevent it." Then all of them prayed that
God would preserve his honor and life and declared that they
would gladly serve him with everything they had. He
commended them to God and departed.

He knew the roads well and therefore came quickly to the
chapel. Since it was already noon, they had brought the girl
out of her prison, taken off all her clothing except her slip,
and tied her hands. The pyre was ready, a fire had been set
beneath it, and Lady Lunete was on her knees in prayer,
asking God to care for her soul, for she was giving up her
life. Just as she had lost all hope of anyone freeing her, her
defender arrived and was pained by the shame and distress
she was suffering because of him. Sir Iwein trusted fully
that God and her innocence would not permit him to fail and
also believed that his companion, the lion, would be of help
in rescuing the girl. Using his spurs, he dashed up as fast as
his horse could run—she would have been lost if he had
come any later—and cried out, "Wicked people, let this girl
alone. I will answer to any charges against her and fight for
her if she needs a champion." Her three accusers were
highly insulted when they heard this, but they moved aside
and made way for the stranger.

He looked around, trying to catch sight of her whom his
secret heart gazed upon all of the time and acknowledged as
its mistress. Soon he saw where she was sitting and almost
lost his senses, as before; they say it is painful to be near the
joy of one's heart and be a stranger. He also saw many noble
ladies of her retinue and heard them lamenting bitterly to
almighty God. "Lord God," they cried, "we beg You to
avenge us on the one who has caused us to lose our dear
comrade. We gained in wealth and esteem because of her.
Now there is no one in the ladies' quarters who dares speak
for us—as our dear friend the faithful Lunete did early and
late—so that our lady will favor us." These words made Sir
Iwein eager for combat. He rode over to Lunete, bade her
stand up, and said, "Lady, show me your tormentors, if they
are here, and tell them to free you at once or they'll learn
what sort of fight I can give them." Seeing that he was

angry, his protector the lion moved up closer to him.

Fear had so disheartened the innocent, noble girl that at first she hardly dared raise her eyes, but then she pulled herself together and spoke, "May God reward you, sir! He knows that I have had to suffer this insult and disgrace through no fault of mine, and I pray that He may give them strength to oppose you only to the extent of my guilt." And she pointed out all three. Then the lord high steward said, "Whoever comes to die because of you is surely foolhardy, but it is only just that he who desires his own death should get it and that even he who is in the wrong should be allowed to fight. The whole country knows of her treachery, of how she betrayed her mistress by causing the lady to disgrace herself. Indeed, sir, I advise you to reconsider. I would really be sorry if we had to take from you both honor and life because of such a disloyal woman. See, there are three of us, and if you aren't a rash boy, you will do well to give up a cause which will cost you your life."

"No matter how you threaten," replied the knight with the lion, "you will still have to fight me or let her go free. The innocent girl swore to me upon oath that she was not guilty of any treachery toward her mistress and that she never gave her false counsel. What if there are three of you? Do you think I am alone? God always stands by Truth; both of them are here with me, and I know they will support me. So there are also three of us, and I have more powerful allies than you."

"If I should dare oppose our Lord God," spoke the steward, "I would surely gain only injury and scorn. Sir, you threaten me with God, but I believe He is more likely to help us than you. However, I see that you do have a companion, this lion of yours. You must command it to go off a way, for no one here is going to fight you two. We aren't worried about the others." "The lion is always with me," answered Sir Iwein. "I didn't bring it just for the combat, but I shall not drive it away from me either. If it attacks you, defend yourself." Then they all cried out together that no one would fight him if he didn't send the lion off, and he would see the girl

burned at once. "I can't let that happen," he said. So the lion
had to go farther away, but it couldn't help looking back
over its shoulder at its master as it went.

So they laid down their words and took up arms for battle.
Mounting quickly, the four rode off in opposite directions to
have room for a charge. Then three men dashed against one
as fast as their horses could take them. In the battle which
followed, Sir Iwein had to defend himself as a wise man who
shrewdly saves his skill and strength for the right moment.
All of his foes broke their spears on him, but he kept his in-
tact and, turning his horse away from them, raced off the
length of a field. Then he whirled about, set his spear firmly
against his chest, as he always did, and charged back. The
lord high steward, who had left his brothers behind in his
eager pursuit, now came at Sir Iwein with his sword. The
knight's spear caught him under the chin and lifted him so
high out of the saddle that he appeared to fly. He lay
stretched out in the sand and made no further attempt to
harm Sir Iwein; the others couldn't hope for aid from him because he was senseless a long time. Both of those who were
left again rode at Sir Iwein and wielded their swords like
true warriors. They were well repaid because each of his
blows was like two of theirs. Still, he surely had need
of strength and vigor since two men are really too much
for one.

The ladies of the court all prayed that God in His mercy
and power would come to their aid, give victory to their
champion, and save the companion who was their comfort.
Well, God is so gracious and kind that He could never refuse
a just prayer that came from so many sweet lips. Those who
fought against Sir Iwein were not cowards, and he was in
great danger. Although they didn't manage to kill him, they
truly pressed him very hard—without taking anything from
his honor, however. Then the steward came to his senses, got
up from the ground, picked up his sword and shield, and ran
to help his brothers. At this, the lion thought it high time to
intervene in the conflict. It quickly charged at him and
fiercely tore at his armor: those watching could see the rings
of mail flying like straw. It overpowered the steward and

mangled him wherever it could get at him. So it was the command of the lion that freed Lady Lunete from him. Its command was death, and she was happy at this, with good reason.

The lord high steward lay lifeless, and the lion sprang furiously at his companions, who had given and received many heavy blows. They were now in great danger and really had to fight for their lives, for Sir Iwein could not drive off the lion and had to let it stay. He had been willing to do without its aid, but was not greatly angered that it rushed to help him; he neither thanked nor reproved it. They attacked from both sides; the man here, the lion there. Their foes too did not hold back: if bravery alone could have preserved them, they would have been safe enough. Each managed to wound the lion, which, however, only caused it to fight more fiercely. Sir Iwein was so distressed to see the lion bleeding that he gave up all restraint and attacked with such fury that his enemies lost both the strength and the will to continue. They were thus defeated, but only after wounding him four times. Still, no one heard him lament his own injuries, just those of the lion.

Now, it was the custom in those days that the accuser was condemned to the same death that the one was to have suffered whom he challenged to a trial by combat, if the results showed the accused to be innocent. The practice was observed also in this case as Sir Iwein's foes were laid on the pyre. The ladies of the court all hurried to be of service to Lady Lunete and, falling at the feet of her champion, gave him their heartfelt thanks; they showed him every honor he could have expected and more than he wanted. Lady Lunete was very happy, for she regained the favor of her mistress, who from then on made amends to her for the grief and distress she had endured although innocent.

It was easy for Sir Iwein to depart, since no one knew who he was except Lady Lunete, whom he had commanded to keep silent. It was strange that she who carried his heart about with her did not recognize him. However, she did urge him to remain, saying, "For God's sake, dear sir, stay here with me so that I can take care of you until you are well. I know that both you and your lion are badly wounded." But the nameless knight replied, "I shall nevermore find rest or happiness until I again have my lady's good will, of which I am unjustly deprived." "I can praise neither the person nor the sentiments," she answered, "of her who denies her favor to such a brave man as you have here shown yourself to be. Unless you have caused her much grief, she isn't wise." "May help never come to me," he replied, "if her wish was not always my command: God grant that she may soon remember me. God knows I shall not tell my trouble to anybody except the one who is already aware of how deeply it pains me." "Does anyone beside you two know about it?" she asked. "No, lady," replied Sir Iwein. "Won't you tell me your lady's name?" she spoke. "Lady, I can't do that either," he answered, "I must first win back her affection." "Then at least tell me who you are," she said. To this he replied, "I want to be known by the lion who travels with me. If she never has mercy on me, I shall always be ashamed of my life and my name and shall never be happy. I am called the knight with the lion, and from now on when you are told anything about a knight whose companion is a lion, you will know that it is I."

"How can it be," asked the lady, "that I have never seen nor heard of you before?" The knight with the lion answered, "You have heard nothing about me because I am not well known. I should have devoted will, life, and wealth to gaining greater fame. However, if my luck is as good as my spirit and intention, I am sure I shall yet perform such deeds that you will know me better." "If you are as noble a man as you appear," she said, "you are worthy of every honor. And if it would do any good, I would repeat my request. I don't think I could bear the shame and disgrace if someone were to see you leaving my land so badly wounded." "God protect you and give you His favor and the esteem of men," he replied. "I must go now." To this the lady responded, "Since you won't accept my aid, I commend you to God, Who can care for you better than I. May He in His kindness soon transform your sorrow to happiness and honor." Sir Iwein departed sadly, saying to himself, "Lady, how little you know that you yourself have the key. And you are the lock and the chest which encloses my joys and honors."

It was now time to ride away. No one accompanied him but Lady Lunete, who went with him for a long way. She then made him a promise which she later kept: she gave him her word that she would never forget him and would see to it that his sorrow came to an end. The good Lady Lunete was so loyal and trustworthy that she was glad to do this. He gave her a thousand thanks.

The wounds of the lion were so severe that it had great difficulty following Sir Iwein along the road. When it could walk no farther, he dismounted, gathered moss and whatever other soft plants he could find, and lined his shield with them. He then placed the lion on it and lifted it onto the horse in front of him. He, too, was in a wretched state and suffered great distress until the road led him to where he saw a castle. Needing rest and care, he turned off toward it and found a squire in front of the closed gate. Reflecting the disposition of his lord, who was noble and kind, the youth welcomed him and offered him food and lodging. And Sir Iwein, who was very tired and weak from the journey, had to accept: a guest who wants to stop with you needs little urging. The gate opened and he was approached by knights and servants who greeted him courteously and were glad to relieve his pain and distress, as their lord had commanded. The latter also came and received him with pleasure, then provided such comforts that one could see by his works that he was good and without fault. They quickly made ready a private room for him and his lion and took off his armor there. His host sent for two of his daughters, very beautiful girls, to whom he commended Sir Iwein that they might apply healing ointment to his wounds and bind them. They were not only skillful but also eager to help and quickly cured both him and his companion. He stayed here for two weeks—until he had fully recovered his strength—before departing.

At this time Death brought suit against a certain Count of Black Thorn with such distressing success that he was lost, for he had to give up both health and life itself to meet the judgment. He left behind two lovely girls, the older of whom wished to seize by force the inheritance which was to have served them both. At this the younger said, "Sister, God forbid that you should do me this injury. I had hoped to have more pleasant rela-

tions with you. You are too unkind, and, if you try to rob me of
my property and position, I shall put up a struggle. Since I am a
woman, I can't fight myself, but you will gain nothing by my not
being a warrior; I shall surely find a man gallant enough to defend me against you. Sister, you must turn over my portion or
get yourself a champion because I am going to King Arthur's
court and shall indeed find there a warrior whose bravery will
protect me from your arrogance."

The wicked sister took note of this and considered what she
would do about it. Cunning as she was, she said nothing but got
to the court first, soon enough to obtain the service of Sir Gawein. And the inexperience of the younger sister, which caused
her to reveal her plan, made her arrive later and find the other
already there. The older one was very pleased with her champion, but Sir Gawein had promised to fight for her only on condition that she not tell anyone. This was at the time of the return
of the queen, whom Meljakanz had carried off with great bold-
ness. It was also when they first heard the story of the giant and
how he had been slain by the knight with the lion. When his
niece told him all about it (at the unknown knight's request),
the good Sir Gawein expressed his heartfelt thanks that it had
been done for his sake, but also lamented bitterly that he didn't
know who the man was, since he had not given his name. He
knew her champion only through the story.

As I told you, when the girl came to the court in search of a
champion (whom no one helped her find), she became greatly
concerned about her property and position, because the one on
whom she had counted said, "Lady, I cannot serve you since I am
very busy with other things I have to do. If you had come to me
sooner, before I had taken on another task, I would have been
ready to aid you." Since she could not get a champion there, she
went at once to King Arthur and said, "I did not want to leave
without saying goodbye to you, even though I cannot find a defender at your court. Still, I shall not give up my rightful inheritance because there is no one here. I have heard of the great
bravery of the knight with the lion and am sure he will help me
if I can learn where he is. If my sister acts justly toward me, I
shall be satisfied. Then she can get by friendly agreement whatever she wants of mine, as long as she goes about it properly. But

I shall not let her take anything against my will without challenge."

However, as soon as the older sister was sure that the best knight at the court would fight for her, she took a solemn oath that she would never share at all. At this, the king said to her, "This is the custom here: whenever one person brings suit against another, the plaintiff must be given forty days to arrange for a combat." She replied that anyone who wanted to fight should do so without delay because she wouldn't wait any longer. But she changed her mind when the king did not think this right, because she had no fear that her sister would bring someone there who would defeat her champion, even if she waited a year. So King Arthur announced that the combat would take place in six weeks.

The younger sister then took leave of the court, prayed that God might take care of her, and rode forth to seek her champion. She travelled far and wide through many lands but did not find either the man or news of where he might be, and at last the aimless journey so exhausted her that she became ill. Still making inquiries, she stopped with one of her relatives, where she told the purpose of her wanderings and lamented her trouble and sickness. Seeing her distress, he kept her there to care for her and, at her request, sent forth in her place his daughter, who continued the search and suffered great hardships in doing so.

Without companions she rode all day and at dusk took a road that led her into a forest. The night was dark and cold, and a storm brought wind and rain. A stouthearted man would have been distressed at this ordeal, to say nothing of a young girl who had never before endured trials of any kind. Unused to such perils, she was badly frightened. As the way became darker and her horse began to sink deeper into the mire, she called on God to consider her need and guide her to a dwelling. Just when she gave herself up for lost, she heard a horn in the distance, and our Lord saw to it that she turned in the direction from which the sound came. A valley led her toward the castle, and the watchman on the parapet caught sight of her at once. A stranger who rides up so late and so weary is easily persuaded to stop for the night if he isn't in a great hurry, and she didn't need to be asked

twice. When they had done everything they could to make her
comfortable and she had all she needed and had finished eating,
her host became eager to hear about her journey and asked what
her mission was. "I am seeking a man I do not know and have
never seen," said the girl, "and I don't even know his name, since
it was never told to me. All I know about him is that he has a
lion. People speak of his great courage, and I need him badly. If
my ordeal is to end, I must find him."

"You were not misled," said her host, "and the one who
praised him didn't lie to you. God sent him to help me, and his
heroism saved me from great distress. I shall always be grateful
to the path that brought him here. He slew a giant who had
burned and laid waste my land, killed two of my children, and
captured and would have hanged four who are still alive. I was
only an object of scorn to him. Then God sent this knight to
avenge me, and while I looked on, he slew the giant right in
front of my gate: the bones are still lying there. The knight
restored my honor; may God watch over him wherever he goes."
The girl was very pleased at this news and said, "Dear sir, do you
know where he went when he left you? If so, please tell me." "I'm
truly sorry, lady, but I don't," he replied. "However, in the morning I'll show you the road he took, and perhaps God will help you
from there on." It was now time to retire.

As soon as it was light, the girl set out after the knight,
following the road which had been pointed out to her. It was the
right way, the one that led to the spring where he had killed the
lord high steward and defeated his brothers. She met people
there who told her about it and advised her that the one for
whom he had slain them could perhaps direct her if she wanted
to know where he had gone. "Tell me, who is it?" she inquired.
"A girl named Lunete," they replied, "who is close by. She is
praying in the chapel there. Ride over and ask her. If she can't
tell you, no one here can." When asked if she knew where the
knight was, Lady Lunete (who liked to do the courtly thing) sent
for her horse and said, "I'll go with you to the place to which I
accompanied him—at his request—when he rode out of the
country after having fought for me here." So she led her there
and spoke thus: "Look, lady, I left him at this place, but he
wouldn't tell me where he intended to go. I lament to God that he

and his lion were so badly wounded that he could not have
travelled very far then. May our Lord preserve his life! He is
everything a knight should be. Truly, I hope for your sake as
well as his that you find him in good health, for he will end all
your troubles. God knows, lady, I would be dead if he hadn't
come to my aid. May you be freed from oppression in like manner. I shall be glad to hear good news of you."

With this they parted, and the girl hastened to continue her
search. She followed the right road and came to the castle in
which Sir Iwein was so well cared for, where he recovered from
his wounds. Riding up to the gate, she saw there a retinue of
knights and ladies that indeed did honor to the lord of the castle.
She went quickly to them and asked if they knew anything
about the knight she sought. Then the lord was kind enough to
come up and greet her pleasantly and offer her lodging. "I am
looking for a man," she said, "and must do without comfort and
rest until I find him. I was directed here." "What is his name?"
he asked. "I was sent to get him," she answered, "and was told no
more about him than that a lion is with him." "He just took leave
of us," he said. "I couldn't persuade him to stay longer. He and
his lion have fully recovered. They both were badly wounded
when they came, but left healthy and in good spirits. If you want
to overtake him soon, you shouldn't wait. Follow the tracks of
the horse carefully, and if you keep to the right road, you will
quickly catch up with him."

There was no further delay. She didn't keep to an amble but
galloped and trotted until she caught sight of him. May you and
I be as happy at seeing each other as she was then! "Mighty and
gracious God," she reflected, "what luck shall I have now that I
have found the man? I have suffered many hardships during
this search and until now have only thought of how happy I
would be to find him, since all my troubles would be over then.
But now that I have caught up with him, I am really worried as
to how he will act toward me. If he declines to help, all my efforts
were in vain." And she whispered this prayer: "Lord God, give
me the words that will serve me best, so he won't think me troublesome and won't refuse me. If either my misfortune or his anger causes me to lose my request, then my finding him will mean
nothing. God give me luck and wisdom!"

Then she quickly rode up beside him and said, "Good day, sir. I have come a long way looking for you so that I could ask a favor. I pray to God that you will grant it." "It is not a matter of favors," he replied. "I shall not refuse help to any good person who really needs it." He wished her well because he could easily see that she had suffered hardships in searching for him. "Lady," he continued, "I am sorry you are in distress, but you needn't worry any longer about it if there is something I can do." At this, she bowed her head in gratitude to him and to God and thanked him with all her heart. "Dear sir," she said, "the request is not for myself but for another, much worthier than I, who sent me after you. Force is being used to wrong her: I'll tell you about it.

"Her father died a short time ago, and her sister, because she is a little older, wants to seize her inheritance and leave her destitute. The lady was barely able to win a delay of five and a half weeks, after which a trial by combat is to decide the matter. If she is not fortunate enough to bring to the trial a champion who will protect her from injustice, her sister will take her legacy. Since everyone praises you, she chose you to save her, and it was neither pride nor laziness that kept her from seeking you herself. She started out, but, sad to say, the hard journey made her sick, and she had to stop on the way at my father's court and go to bed. He sent me on in her stead, and I implore you now just as she asked me to. Sir, she bade me urgently remind you that, since God has so honored you that you are more famous than many other knights, you should now honor God and womankind and thus show yourself courtly and wise. Deign to spread your fame, for her sake and your own, by saving her wealth and adding to your esteem. In God's name, tell me your decision." "The messenger hasn't forgotten a single thing," he said. "The old saying is true: who sends forth a good spokesman attains his goal. I can indeed tell by the messenger whether the lady should be defended and shall gladly do her will as far as my strength permits. Now ride ahead and show me the way, and I'll follow you."

In this manner the girl was received and her doubts and fears vanished. They passed the time while riding across the heath by telling each other many stories and the latest news until they saw near the road a castle which was well suited for people who need a lodging for the night, as they did. The castle stood alone on a hill, but down below was a small market town, into which they rode. However, all the people standing or seated by the road greeted them so rudely they might easily have been frightened by the hostile glances and the fact that some turned their backs on them. Others said: "You are coming at the wrong time, we don't need you"; "If you knew how things are here, you would ride on"; "You won't get much respect in this place. Who do you think will welcome you?"; "Why did you take it on yourself to come here? Who wants you? You would be better off someplace else"; "The wrath of God sent you here to punish you. You aren't welcome."

On hearing all this, the knight with the lion replied, "What do these threats and reproaches mean: what did I do to deserve them? If I ever angered you, it was done unknowingly. I am telling the truth when I say that I didn't come to harm you and shall leave as the friend of all of you if I can. Dear people, if you receive all strangers as you have me, it must be really disheartening to one who needs your help." As he turned into the road up to the castle, his way took him past a lady (one not born in the town) who heard his displeasure and beckoned to him from a distance. When he approached, she said, "Don't be so annoyed; the people are saying these things with good intentions. They are concerned about your honor and this noble lady, for you will never be able to save your life if you ride up to the castle. They don't talk like this because they are unfriendly but because they would rather you avoided the castle and rode on. And we have been issued a decree, which can be disobeyed only with the loss of life and property, that no one outside the castle gate is to take in a guest, so you can't get lodging down here. May God protect you, since I know very well that you will risk your life if you go there. I advise you to turn around and ride on."

"Perhaps it would be better if I followed your advice," answered Sir Iwein, "but it is too late. Where would I go? I must spend the night here." "By God, I would be happy to see you come back out of there with honor," spoke the lady, "but, I'm sorry to say, that can't be." So he rode farther, until the gatekeeper saw him and beckoned to him, saying, "Come on, knight, come on. I assure you they will be very glad to see you here, although that won't help you." He didn't keep him waiting after

the greeting, but opened the gate at once and received him with
many threats. He looked at the knight with the malice of a
treacherous man and said, "I took good care to get you in: now
see how you are going to get out," and barred the gate after him.

However, since he saw no danger before or behind the gate,
the knight paid no attention to what was said. Once inside, he
noticed a large building which appeared to be a dwelling for poor
people and, looking through a window, saw that it was a work-
house in which some three hundred women were busy. They
were thin, poorly clad, and young. Many were weaving such
things as are made of silk and gold, and others were at embroi-
dery frames, doing fine needlework. Of those not skilled at
either, some sorted thread, some wound it, some beat flax, some
scraped it, some combed it, some spun, some sewed. Yet all suffered from want, since their work brought them hardly enough
to preserve life and left them suffering constantly from hunger
and thirst. They were pale, gaunt, almost dead, and showed
their great need in dress as well as in body. There was seldom
meat or fish on their hearth, for their host neither feasted nor
honored them: they struggled with direst want.

The women also saw the knight, which made their sorrow
much greater. Their arms sank down with shame, and tears
welled up in their eyes and fell onto their clothing, so bitter was
their pain that a stranger had seen how needy they were. Since
he observed no one else around, he wanted to ask the gatekeeper
about the wretched women, but when he turned back toward the
gate, the knave greeted him with a knavish mouth and said as
knavishly as he could: "Do you want to go out, Sir Stranger? It
can't be done; the gate is barred. There are other plans for you.
Before the gate is opened for you, you shall get your proper de-
serts and leave in a quite different manner. Before then they
shall prepare all sorts of infamy for you and thus teach you the
manners of this court. How God forsook you when I lured you in
here! You will depart in shame."

"You all can threaten as much as you like," said the knight
with the lion, "but if I meet with no greater danger than that, I'll
live forever. Why do you bar your gate? If I were on the other
side, I would still ride in again. I came back to ask a question.
Tell me, friend, what is the story of these poor women? Their

manner and appearance make it seem that they would be very pretty if they were happy and rich." The other refused to answer, saying, "I'll tell you nothing. Do you think, Sir Stranger, that your idle questions don't annoy me? You are wasting your time." "I am sorry for that," replied the knight and turned away with a laugh, as one will do who doesn't want to get into a quarrel with a boor. He thought the gatekeeper was just amusing himself.

He then went around the building from wall to wall until he found the doorway, which he entered. However much the spirits of the women were depressed by poverty, they yet remained composed and bowed to him from all sides, letting their work rest while he sat with them. The fine manners of their birth required this. He also noticed that there was no needless talking, such as is common when many women are together, for here prudence and good breeding dwelt together with want. They often blushed with shame when he offered his service, and while he was with them, their eyes became sad and wet. "If you don't mind," he said, "I would like to ask about your station and families because, if I haven't lost my wits, you were not born poor. I can readily see that you are deeply ashamed of your poverty and judge from this, since those who are used to it from childhood are not so pained by it as you appear to be. Don't tell me any more or less than just what your condition is. Did you come to this life through birth or through misfortune?"

"We shall be glad to tell you of our birth and our present condition," answered one of them. "We lament to God and all good people about how we were robbed of respect and esteem and brought to this wretched state. Sir, our land is called the Island of Maidens and is far away. Because he was young and rash, the lord of the country decided to ride forth in search of adventure. To our misfortune, his way led him here, as yours did, and his fate was just as yours will be. For it won't help to refuse: tomorrow you must fight two servants of the devil who are so mighty that if you had the strength of six men, it would be nothing against them. God can save you if He wishes—nothing is too hard for Him—but otherwise there is no hope for you. Tomorrow we must see you in the same distress in which many others have been before now.

"It was thus that my lord rode up here and was to have fought them. He was noble and brave but only eighteen and not yet at full strength, so that unwillingly he had to yield without a struggle. He would have been killed if he had not ransomed himself from these accursed giants by taking an oath of fealty and giving hostages and security as pledges that he would pay tribute: thirty girls, whom he had to send them every year as long as he and they lived, under the condition, however, that if anyone were to defeat these two, we were to be set free. Sad to say, there is no hope of this because they are not only very strong but also so fearless that no man will ever conquer them.

"We are the tribute and have a wretched life. Our youth is passed in misery because those to whom we are subject are quite without decency and will not allow us to profit at all by our hard labor. We simply have to endure whatever comes. With silk and gold we make the finest clothing in the world. But what good does it do us? We don't live any better. We have to strain hands and arms to the limit in order to earn barely enough to keep from starving. I'll tell you what we are paid, and you say who could get rich from it. We are given only four pence of each pound earned, which is too little pay for food and clothing, so we are always in need of both. They have become rich from our earnings, and we live in misery."

Touched by their misfortune, the knight sighed deeply and said, "May God in His mercy reward you ladies for your hard life with His favor and honor. I am sorry about your distress, so much so, I assure you, that I would be very glad to set you free if I could. I'll look for the people who live in the castle and see how they act toward me. No matter how fearful the affair may be, with God's help I hope to come through unharmed." With this, he commended them to God, and they voiced many prayers that God might bless him.

He went farther and saw a beautiful hall, which he and the girl approached, looking for someone, but found nobody there. After searching it carefully, he took a side path which led to a road that went past the hall. Soon he came to stairs which brought him to a very large park, the finest he had ever seen. There he saw an old knight resting on a bed with which the goddess Juno in her greatest glory would have been pleased, while pretty flowers and fresh grass spread odors around him: it was a splendid place to lie. A lady (his wife, I suppose) was sitting in front of him. Considering their advanced age, the two could not have been more handsome nor have conducted themselves more graciously. In front of them both sat a girl who, so I'm told, could read French very well. She whiled away the time for them, often making them laugh: they thought whatever she read was charming because she was their daughter. It is right that one should give the crown of honor to her who has good manners, beauty, noble birth, youth, wealth, modesty, kindness, and prudence. She had these and, indeed, everything else one could wish in a woman, which made it a joy to listen to her read.

When they saw the stranger, the lord and the lady hurried toward him while he was still some distance away and greeted him as warmly as any host would receive a welcome guest. Then their daughter quickly helped him off with his armor—no stranger could want better treatment—and clothed him in pure white, finely pleated linen and a velvet, ermine-lined jacket, such as looks nice with a shirt. He didn't need an overcoat because the evening was warm. She led him by the hand to the finest turf in the park and sat down there with him. He then learned that she was friendly and gifted as well as youthful and charming and would have sworn that one could never find a young girl with more pleasant speech or better manners. She could almost have so turned the head of an angel with them that he would have given up heaven for her, and she struck such a blow at the loyalty the knight bore in his heart that it would have been driven out if any woman's kindness had been able to do this. It would have been better if he had never seen her, since parting caused him so much pain. Except for his wife, he never met a woman before or later who was as lovely or spoke with such charm.

When the four had split up so quickly into two groups, they did this according to age and spirit. I am quite sure that their wishes and thoughts were different. The young ones secretly longed for true love, were happy with their youth, and spoke of the summer's beauty and of how joyfully they would like to spend their lives. The old pair, however, talked of their age, of the coming winter (which most likely would be very cold), of fox-fur hats to protect their heads from frost, and discussed household affairs: what should be spent for their needs and comfort. Meanwhile it became late, and a messenger came to say that dinner was ready.

When they went to eat, the family showed great respect for the stranger; indeed, no host ever honored a guest more highly. He received a full measure of esteem and attention to his every want, which was proper and well deserved. At the same time, he was thinking: "Everything is going all right thus far, yet I am afraid I shall have to pay very dearly for this much too friendly reception, just as was promised by the rogue (my host's gate-keeper) who let me into the castle and was suggested by the story the ladies told me. But be of good courage and don't worry: what is destined will happen to you and not a thing more. This is certain."

After they had finished eating and had sat talking a short time, the beds of the travelers were made ready in a separate room, for their greater comfort. Whoever thinks it strange that a girl not of kin should sleep so near the knight without his touching her is not aware that an upright man can deny himself everything he should—although, God knows, there are too few of these. The night passed peacefully: God grant them in the morning better news than the knight expected! As soon as it was day he attended a votive mass of the Holy Spirit and got ready to depart. But when he wanted to take leave of his host, the old man said, "All of the knights who have come to this castle have observed a custom of mine which brought them into great danger. There are two giants here, and each of my guests must fight them: what a pity that no one yet has defeated them! However, to the man lucky enough to overcome them both, I would have to give my daughter, and if he should outlive me, he would win high position as well as this entire land, since I have no other children. Sad to say, my daughter cannot marry until they are conquered. Risk your life, knight. Perhaps you are poor; if so, become rich or die. Maybe you will be the very man to win the prize. It often happens that one person defeats two."

The knight answered him as if he were faint-hearted: "Your daughter is lovely, noble, and rich, and I am by no means suitable for her: a lady should marry a lord. And when I take a wife, it will be one in keeping with my station. I don't want your daughter and I also don't want ever to risk my life for a woman in such a reckless manner as to let myself be so shamefully killed without a chance of defense, because two can always defeat one. I would be in real danger fighting even a single giant." "You are a coward," said his host. "I know why you talk about not being good enough for my daughter: you refuse her only because you are afraid. You had better fight, for that alone can save you." "Sir," replied the knight, "it is distressing that one must pay for your food and lodging with his life. Yet I suppose I might as well fight now as put it off, since I shall have to anyway."

He waited no longer but put on his armor and sent for his horse. It had received better care than he had ever given it; still, God should not reward him who took such pains because it was not done to please the owner. Often things get turned around so that one person helps another when the intent was to harm him. It is only just that the pay for the good deed should be small when done against one's will, and the knight doesn't need to thank the residents of the castle for looking after his horse when they expected it to stay there with them. If they were mistaken, I truly can't say that I am sorry.

The guest was soon ready, and the giants came, prepared for battle. They could easily have frightened an army. They were well protected with armor that left only their heads, arms, and legs exposed, and each carried a club that crushed everything it struck and had already killed many people. But when they saw the powerful lion standing by its master, great jaws open wide and long claws tearing at the ground, they said, "Sir, what does the lion want? It looks as if it were threatening us with this fierce manner. There won't be any combat unless the lion is locked up. If it fought with you, that would be two against two." "My lion is always with me," replied Sir Iwein. "I like to have it beside me and shall never order it to leave. I didn't bring it to take part in the combat, but since you are my enemies, I would be glad to see you harmed, whether by man or beast." However, they insisted at once that they would not fight him unless he took the lion away, so he had to do this. It was put into a shed but could see the fight in the courtyard through a crack in the wall.

The two huge men attacked. May God protect the stranger, because he had never been in such danger: it was not equal combat. His shield was soon beaten to pieces, and nothing he wore protected him much from the clubs: his helmet and the rest of his armor were crushed as if made of straw. But the knight's skill and bravery saved him from death for a while, and now and then he paid them back with a telling blow from his sword. When his comrade, the lion, heard and saw the fierce blows, it was greatly disturbed by the danger he was in but could find no way to get out. It searched everywhere and at last found a decaying foundation beam. It then tore away wood and earth with claws and teeth until there was a hole large enough for its escape, which quickly doomed one of the giants. May God destroy them both! It repaid its master there for the danger he had once braved on its account by sinking sharp claws into the giant's back and dashing him to the ground. God's judgment was carried out as the lion bit and tore him wherever he was exposed until he cried for help.

His companion didn't delay any longer but left the knight and charged at the lion to kill it. However, its master wouldn't let this happen, and just as the lion had relieved him, so he now came to its aid, which was indeed right. As soon as that servant of the devil turned his back, the knight—with God's blessing—gave him many wounds: in the arms and legs and wherever he was not protected by armor. And the one on the ground could not come to support him, since the lion had so robbed him of strength and sense that he lay as if dead. Both lion and knight attacked the other giant and soon killed him although he fought bravely, striking many mighty blows even after there was no chance of help from his comrade. The latter, who was still alive, had to yield and swear fealty, and the knight, for the sake of God, let him live. May God be praised for the good fortune which came in place of the disgrace and scorn threatened by the gatekeeper!

After the victory his host offered him daughter and land, but the knight said, "If you knew how fully the love for another has captured my heart, you would be glad not to have me marry your daughter, because I can never be faithful to any woman except her whose absence makes me sad." "You will marry my daugh-

ter or become a prisoner," was the reply. "You are lucky that I
am so ready to give her to you. If you had good sense as well as
good fortune, you would be asking for her instead of my asking
you to take her." "You would be cheated if I did," spoke the
knight, "and I'll tell you why. In a few days I must fight a battle
before King Arthur at his court. If she became my wife and I
were killed, she would share my disgrace." "Go where you
want," answered his host. "I don't care. I am sorry I ever offered
you my daughter and shall never do so again."

Undisturbed by the angry words, the knight said, "Dear sir,
may I urge you to remember now your honor as a nobleman and
keep your vow. Since I gained the victory here, you should let all
of your prisoners go." "That is right," answered his host and
freed them at once. He kept the knight there a week in order to
get fine clothing and good riding horses for the ladies. They were
now so well tended that they became healthy again and in this
short time became the most beautiful group of women the
knight had ever seen: all because of the brief rest and care. He
then rode away with them and brought them to safety, as a
courtly man would. When he left them, they prayed earnestly
(which was right) that God might grant His grace, man's esteem, a long life, and finally His kingdom to their lord and comfort, who had saved them from great distress.

Well, who could menace the knight now, when he had
emerged from the combat with his lion uninjured? He at once
continued the journey to meet the girl for whom he had promised to fight, the one who had been left behind sick by her cousin. The latter showed him the right roads, and they found the
girl in the care of the cousin's father. Plaintiff and champion did
not delay, because the day set for the combat was so close that
they had just enough time to make the trip. They arrived
promptly at the place of combat and found the girl's adversary,
her sister, already there. Sir Gawein, who had asked to remain
unknown, had earlier stolen away and concealed himself after
telling everyone that he could not watch the fight because of
other affairs. So when he secretly returned with different weapons and armor, no one knew him but the older sister, whom he
had told of his plan.

King Arthur sat waiting with all his retinue, who were eager to see how the fight went, as Sir Iwein and the girl also rode up. The lion was not with them, because the knight did not want it present at the combat and had left it behind. No one there knew who he was. When the two champions rode into the ring, everyone thought it would be very sad if no way were found to keep one of them from being slain. There would be good reason to lament him a long time, for all agreed that they had never seen two knights so perfect in appearance and manners. His retinue, therefore, asked the king that he request the older sister to share with the younger for God's sake. When he did so, however, she refused so abruptly that he had to give up the attempt. She knew the strength of her champion and was sure that he would win the combat for her.

When King Arthur saw that the sisters would not make peace with each other, he ordered that the ring be cleared of all but the champions. It was hard to watch two such fine knights fight, for an upright man does not like to see a man die, even though he must if another is to live. If I were to adorn the battle between these noble knights with great art, what good would it do? You have already heard so much about the bravery of both that you will readily believe they didn't act like cowards on this day and again proved that there has never been two men who could fight better for a worldly prize. That is why they wore the crown of knightly honor, to which each wanted to add now at the cost of the other. I lament bitterly to God that the closest friends of the time should contend: if either kills the other and afterward learns whom he has slain, he will never cease to mourn. If only both or neither could win, or if they were only to recognize each other—that would be the best thing for their enmity. They weren't strangers of the heart but of the eyes, and neither knew that his foe was the best friend he had ever had.

Since the combat must take place, it is well to begin quickly. This is the place and they have the will, so why delay? The horses, too, were in good shape, and they did not need to wait because of them. To make room for a charge, they rode away from each other to the edge of the circle, which was a good 125 paces wide, for they were to start the battle mounted. They weren't just beginners, they knew all about combat. How well they could fight, both mounted and on foot! It had been their pastime from childhood on, which could indeed be seen here. And let me tell you truly that habit will teach a timid man to fight better than a bold warrior who has not practiced. These two were strong and so skillful that they could have taught this art; truly they were the best at it of all the knights then living. They waited no longer but spurred their horses, and those who were in fact comrades dashed at each other like mortal enemies.

It seems to me, and others as well, impossible perhaps that love and hate could take up quarters and dwell together in the same vessel. But if it never happened before, it did here, and neither love nor hate was forced out.

"Friend Hartmann, I think you are wrong. Why do you say that love and hate are living in one vessel? Think it over. Love and hate would be too crowded there: hate leaves when it sees true love, and Lady Love fades away wherever hate dwells."

I'll explain how earnest love and bitter hate remained in a narrow vessel. Each of their hearts was quite narrow and yet hate and love dwelt there together, but a wall separated them so that hate did not know about love, which otherwise would have caused it such distress that hate would have had to leave the vessel in disgrace, and hate will still do so if it finds Lady Love in its dwelling. Ignorance was the wall which divided their hearts so that their seeing eyes were blind although they were good friends: it wanted one comrade to kill the other. If he had done this and later learned who it was, he never would have been happy again from that time on. His success would have become a curse and his sorrow would never have ended, even when fortune had been most kind. Whoever had won the victory would have been defeated by it. All his hopes of happiness would have brought him misery. He would have hated what he loved and lost when he won.

The horses galloped swiftly, and at just the right moment, the champions lowered their spears and braced them against their chests to steady them. The spears were held neither too high nor too low but exactly as they should be, for each wanted to unhorse the other. Both spears struck the spot above the edge of the shield and below the helmet, where the man aims who knows how to fell his opponent. This was made clear, because the knights were knocked backwards so hard that they came closer

to falling than ever before; they barely saved themselves, remaining in the saddle only because the spears broke. They had
come together with such force that the spear shafts splintered
into hundreds of pieces: everyone said he had never seen a finer
joust.

It was followed by many more. A host of nimble squires ran
about, each carrying two or three spears and calling loudly. One
could hear nothing but the resounding cry, "A spear! A spear!
This is broken, bring another," until all the spears they could
get were used up. If they had then fought with swords while
mounted—which neither wanted to do—the poor horses would
have been killed, so in order to avoid such brutality, they had to
continue the battle on foot. They didn't want to strike the
horses, who had done nothing to them, but each other.

I'll tell you how the two practiced warriors fought when they
came together. Each spared the other's armor, but neither his
own sword nor the other's shield: this is what they were after,
what was roughly treated. Both thought, "I'm wasting my
efforts as long as he has the shield in front of him: with it he's
safe enough," so they cut the shields to pieces and didn't even
bother to aim blows at the lower legs, which were not protected
by the shields.

Without guarantor or pawn, they lent each other more
mighty blows than I can tell about and were repaid at once. It is
good to pay loans promptly because he who does this can borrow
easily whenever he wishes. They had to be careful about it, for
the one who borrows and doesn't repay is often punished. They
were afraid they would suffer if they took without returning,
since it often goes hard with him who defaults. Indeed, they
wouldn't have gotten off easily if the loans had not been repaid,
so each gave back in such a manner that his credit was maintained. They had to do it quickly to avoid the rebukes of death
and those whose trade it is to sing abusive songs about debtors.
They gave back with open hands but did not need to send for
more money because they had brought onto the field both loan
and interest; they repaid more and sooner than was requested.
Careless idleness pleases neither God nor men, and no one falls
into this state except the man who fails to meet the claims on
him.

Who wants to gain honor must direct all his thoughts to winning some prize, so he will keep busy in a manner that passes
the time pleasantly and brings him praise. They had done this
and had not spent their lives in idleness. Both of them were
quite unhappy when a period went by without their gaining any
return from their trade. The two were widely known as shrewd
usurers who lent out their goods in a strange manner. They
made a profit, like other merchants do, but their methods were
so different that although they became rich thereby, anyone
else would have been ruined. They made loans in the hope of not
being repaid; however, just see how one can get rich from such
earnings. With spear and sword they lent thrusts and slashes, of
which no one could pay back even half, and thus their fame and
honor increased. They were eager for business and never turned
down a chance to exchange their dangerous labor for fame. Still,
they had never before received such full and prompt payment as
now, for they dealt no single blow that was not returned at once.
And their shields, which were unwillingly offered as security for
their lives, were soon hewn away from their hands. Then they
had to pawn their armor. At last their bodies, too, were not
spared but also used as security. Their helmets were cut to
pieces so that they quickly received many wounds (none mortal)
and their mail began to redden with blood.

This fearful battle started early in the morning and lasted a
long time. By mid afternoon weariness had robbed them of
strength until neither could strike blows powerful enough to
cause injury. At last it seemed to them that the combat did them
no credit, and they stopped fighting. Both were glad to part and
sit down until their strength returned. After a short rest they
sprang up and rushed at each other with renewed desire and vig-
or. The former conflict was nothing compared to that which began. If their blows had been mighty before, they were mightier
now and of greater number. And although many battle-tried
warriors watched the fight, no one's eye was so keen and wise
that he would have been able to say on oath which one had done
better this day by a hair. There was never a more equal contest.

After a while everyone began to worry about their lives and
fame and wanted to part the champions if it could be done properly. They started talking about this because they would have

been distressed if either had been killed or dishonored. By reasoning and urging, the king tried to find some pity in the older girl, the one who had refused to share any of the inheritance with her sister. However, his pleas were in vain, and he was rebuffed so rudely that he could not continue. But the younger girl was troubled at seeing the danger of the brave knights and, when no one found a way to stop the fight, did what she could. The noble and lovely, sensible and modest, sweet and fine girl, whose gentle nature held nothing unpleasing, smiled with red and charming lips at her sister and said, "It would be better if both our land and I went up in flames than that a knight of such merit should suffer death or loss of honor because of me. Take my inheritance with my good wishes: I willingly grant you the victory and the land. Since I can't have it, I truly would rather it go to you than anyone else. Let the combat stop. Their lives are worth more than mine. It is better that I be poor than that either of them should lose his life because of me. I withdraw my claim in your favor."

Everyone who heard praised her intent. They advised and implored the king for God's sake to ask the older girl to give the younger a third, or even less, of the inheritance, for the life of one or both of the knights was at stake if they were not parted. Perhaps she would have agreed if the king had asked, but he was so angry at her because of her hard heart that he would not. He was loath to deny the younger sister's request, since he thought her very noble, but after all she had placed the matter before his court.

The good knights had fought with honor to the end of the long day with many valiant blows, and their lives were still in the balance when night fell and darkness hindered the conflict. In the end, it was night that parted them, and they put off further combat until the next day. Each knew well the other's strength and by this time had had enough of his opponent, and they could leave off now without discredit to themselves. They acted then as right-thinking men have always done, for whatever pain an upright man may suffer from another, he will not hate his adversary if the latter is not simply wanton in trying to kill him; indeed, he will like him better than a worthless person who never harmed him. The truth of this was seen with these two.

Sir Iwein began to confide in his opponent since he (both of them, in fact) would have been greatly pleased to find out who the other was.

"Now that we have stopped our hostile contest," he spoke, "I can say what I wish. I have always been much fonder of the bright day—which brought me many joys, as it does to everyone—than of the night. Day is cheerful and lovely while night is dismal and unpleasant, for it makes the heart sad. Day is the time for weapons and brave deeds while night requires sleep. Until now I have loved day above all, but, noble knight, you have truly quite changed my views. Cursed be the day! From now on I shall hate it because it almost robbed me of all respect. Thank God for night! If I grow old in honor, I shall owe this to it. Don't you think I have good cause to regret and lament the day? If it had lasted three blows longer, you would have won and I would be dead. Only this lovely night saved me. Rest will give me new strength so that I can fight on the hard day ahead. But now I can't help but worry about it, because if God doesn't somehow deliver me, I shall again have to confront the greatest knight I ever met, you. May God be merciful; He knows I have good reason to worry. God save my life and honor; I never feared for them so much before. And let me say this to you: I have never dealt with a man whom I was so eager to know as you. It would surely not demean you if you were to tell me your name."

"It would surely not demean me to tell it to you," said Sir Gawein. "I think as you do. Sir, you spoke up just as I was about to, and if you had been silent, I would have said the very things you said. What you love, I love, and what you fear also worries me. I shall always hate to think of this day which has passed, because it brought me greater danger than I had ever known. Truly, no one ever so robbed me of the strength to fight; if you had seen well enough to strike two more blows before nightfall, I would have had to concede you the victory. I could hardly wait for darkness. As much as I have fought, I have never been in such danger until today, and I am afraid I shall suffer shame or death from you tomorrow. We have the same concern. And I assure you that, because of your valor, I am happy to grant you every honor which does not cost me too much. My heart is filled with grief that I must try to harm you, for as long as it doesn't discredit me,

I wish you everything you desire. God knows you deserve it. I
wish these two girls had what they wanted so that we could treat
each other in a friendly manner. I'll tell you my name: it is Gawein."

"Gawein?"

"Yes."

"I should have guessed it from the beating I took today! With
many hostile blows you vented your wrath on one who is your
devoted servant. I am sure that I would have been spared all this
pain if I had told my name in time, for we once knew each other
well. Sir, I am Iwein." The two then were both joyful and sad:
joyful to have found each other, very sad that they had caused
each other to suffer. But sadness quickly left the vessel of their
heart, taking hate with it, and joy and love reigned there. They
could easily see the change in each other because they threw
away their swords and ran to one another. No one was ever happier, and I don't know if anybody else can have such joy as God
gave them there. They kissed each other a thousand times: on
eyes, cheeks, and lips.

The king and queen were greatly surprised, but pleased, to
see the friendly embraces and hurried up to them at once. Although they soon found out, nobody there knew who either
champion was, since the helmets and the darkness concealed
their faces and the fury of the struggle had so changed their
voices that no one would have known them if they had not given
their names. "Oh!" cried Sir Iwein, "Cursed be this day and the
sword with which I struck you. Sir Gawein, my dear lord, what
more can I say than that I bow before you as your knight and
your servant? That is my will and is fitting. You have so often
honored me and have so well directed my affairs that I have
gained much more fame in many lands than I would have otherwise. If, in return, I could honor you as you deserve, I would
always be happy. But I can't do so other than to be your Iwein, as
always, except for this day, which I can indeed call the most bitter of the year, because truly neither my hand nor my sword
ever were worthy of striking you. I curse the sword and the day,
but my unskilled hand shall be its own pledge that it will make
amends by serving you as long as I live. Sir Gawein, you could
not gain better compensation, for it has discredited me and in-

creased your fame. Its defense was such that you were the victor. I swear fealty to you because God knows I lost. I leave here as your prisoner."

"No, my dear comrade and lord," replied Sir Gawein, "my renown shall not increase at your expense. I'll be glad to do without fame which discredits my friend. Moreover, why should I deceive myself? No matter what honor I might claim, they all saw what happened between us. I yield to you because I was defeated." "Perhaps you think I submitted just for your sake," said Sir Iwein, "but if you were the least known to me of any man in Russia, I would give up before I would confront you again, so it is right for me to yield." "No, lord and comrade, I yield to you," answered Sir Gawein. And the friendly, but earnest, strife went on like this a long time, while the king and his retinue asked each other the meaning of the friendship which followed so closely the enmity they had just seen.

It was quickly explained to the king when his nephew, Sir Gawein, spoke up, "Sir, we shall be glad to tell you about it so you won't think us cowards and no one will fancy that we want to avoid further combat by some ruse. We were once comrades, which, sad to say, we did not know today until this moment. Until he asked my name, I, your nephew Gawein, fought against him whom I am more eager to serve than anyone in the world. When he learned it, he gave his own, and the enmity was over. We are now in full accord. It is my friend Iwein. And, believe me, if he had had more daylight, his bravery and my unjust cause would have put me in great danger. The girl for whom I fought is in the wrong and her sister in the right. As God has always helped the just, I would have died at his hand if night had not intervened. Since I have had this misfortune, I much prefer that my friend has only defeated and not killed me."

Sir Iwein objected to these words and blushed painfully that his friend should praise him so highly. He refused to accept the honor but showed that he could speak even more ably than Sir Gawein, and a peaceful contest began. There was a great deal of talk as each tried to increase the fame of the other at his own expense. This pleased the king, who said, "You must let me settle the matter: I'll make a decision which will do justice to both of you and be a credit to me as well." And so the case was turned over to him. He sent for the two girls and said, "Where is the girl who, through arrogance alone, refused to give a sister her portion of the inheritance which their father left to both?" "Here I am," said the older one quickly. When she thus misspoke, admitting that she was wrong, King Arthur was pleased and called on everyone there to be witnesses to what she had said. "Lady," he went on, "you have confessed and have done this in front of so many people that you cannot disavow it. You must return to her what you have taken if you abide by the judgment of this court."

"By God, no, lord!" she replied. "You can dispose over life and property, but a woman can easily say something she shouldn't, and whoever uses our own words to condemn us will have a great deal to punish. One must make allowances every day for the foolish things we say—which are sometimes harsh (but guileless) and deceitful (though without enmity)—because, sad to say, we don't know any better. You should go by your law and not be arbitrary, even though I may have said the wrong thing." "I shall let you have what is yours," he said, "and your sister have what is hers. The decision about the combat has been left to me, and your noble sister with simple trust has also placed her case in my hands. Justice requires that she receive her portion. If she and I agree, you will come out of the dispute without honor and disgraced, since my nephew Gawein asserts that he was defeated. On the other hand, it would serve your fame and fortune if you would give her portion to her willingly." He said this because he knew she was so hardhearted and stubborn that neither kindness nor a sense of justice would move her, only force or fear.

Frightened by his threat, she said, "Do no more nor less than seems right to you. I agree to give it to her since you insist that I must. I'll share both lands and subjects with her, and you can be the guarantor." "So be it," replied the king. As the matter was left to him, it ended well: pledge and surety were given that the younger sister would receive her portion. When this was finished, the king said, "Nephew Gawein, take off your armor, and let Sir Iwein do the same, for you both are in real need of rest." They did as he commanded.

The lion, which (as you have heard) had been locked up, now

broke out and started on its master's trail at a run. When the people saw him racing toward them across a field, they were badly frightened, and no one held his ground. Men and women had started to flee for their lives when Sir Iwein called: "It won't hurt you. It is my friend and is looking for me." Not until then did they know that he was the famous knight with the lion who had killed the giant and, so they had heard, had performed other wondrous deeds. "My friend," said Gawein, "I have good reason to grieve the rest of my life at having given you such poor thanks for this great favor you did me. You killed the giant for my sake, so my niece said joyfully when she came to me with your message. She told me that the knight with the lion did it because of me but would not let her know his name. I then bowed in all directions, not knowing to whom or where he was, since I wanted to thank the one who had faced great danger for my sake. And if death does not prevent me, I shall fully repay him. I can see by the lion that it was you." Then the lion ran up to its master and showed him its joy and devotion in every way a dumb beast can.

A resting place was made ready at once for the two knights, and their wounds were treated here by doctors for whom Sir Gawein sent. In addition, King Arthur and the queen saw to it that they had good care all of the time. Therefore, they did not have to stay long in the infirmary before they were fully healed. After Sir Iwein was again strong and healthy in body, his spirit still suffered from many almost mortal wounds because of his love for his wife. He felt as if he would soon die if she did not save him at once with help that only she could give. Suddenly the pangs of love forced this idea on him: "No matter how I look at it, I can think of no other way to win her affection than to go to the spring and pour water on it again and again. If I suffer from it, well, I am used to suffering and would rather bear it a short time than the rest of my life. I am always greatly troubled, and only when she is, too, can I force her to return my love."

Accompanied by his lion, he slipped away so that no one—at the court or elsewhere—noticed him and caused such a frightful storm that everybody in the nearby castle expected to perish. "Damned be he forever who first settled this land!" cried all the people there. "A man can subject us to this distress and insult

whenever he wants. There are many wretched places in the
world, but no house was ever built at a worse spot than this."
There was such destruction to the forest, and the tumult of the
raging, roaring storm lasted so long that everyone was beside
himself. "Mistress," said Lady Lunete, "you must find out right
away where you can get a man who will put a stop to this ruin
and misery for you. You'll have to search abroad because, God
knows, there is no one here to help. You could suffer no greater
disgrace than to let the man who has been insulting you so ride
away now without a struggle of any kind. It will happen again
tomorrow: if you don't take care of the matter you will nevermore live in peace." "I bewail my misfortune to you who knows
my affairs better than anyone else," replied her mistress. "Can
you tell me what to do?"

"Lady," said the girl, "you surely have an adviser who is better suited. I am only a woman and would be more foolish than a
child if I presumed to give advice like a wise man. I'll suffer,
along with the others here, whatever I have to suffer until the
day we see who of your retinue comes to your aid, takes this burden on himself, and is able to protect us. Maybe it will happen,
but I don't expect so." "Don't talk like that," was the reply. "I
have no hope of finding such a man in my retinue. Now what is
your best advice?" "If only someone knew," answered the girl,
"where the knight is who killed the giant and saved me from a
shameful death by freeing me from the stake right here before
your eyes. If he could be found and would agree to come, it
couldn't be better. But I know one thing very well: as long as his
lady is unkind to him, no one can persuade him to go any place
unless one promises—in return for his aid to you—to make a
great effort and use every means to help him win back his lady's
love." "I'll devote my life, my wealth, and all the wisdom God
grants me," said the lady, "and drive away her anger if I can.
Here is my hand on it."

"Both you and your entreaties are charming," spoke Lady
Lunete. "What noble lady could refuse such lovely lips if you
were to implore her earnestly? If you really mean it, he will
surely gain her favor, but I must insist that you take an oath to
give him this aid." Lady Lunete had an oath ready that stressed
much that could benefit him whom she was going forth to seek.

"Lady," she said, "I must phrase the oath so carefully that no one can accuse me of treachery. He for whom I shall be looking is a very staunch man who will need staunch words. If you want to send for him and will live up to the words I use in the oath, then, lady, repeat it after me." Her mistress placed her fingers on a reliquary and swore: "If the knight who journeys with the lion comes and helps me out of this trouble, I shall in all honesty devote my power and mind to regain for him his lady's love. May God and these holy saints in like manner help me to win eternal bliss." Nothing was left out here which was needful to him whom the girl wanted to bring back with her.

Lady Lunete was glad to undertake the journey and set out in high spirits, although at the time she had no idea where the knight was. However, she was soon lucky, for she found him beside the spring. She knew him by the lion, and her lord could tell that it was she while Lunete was still a long way off. He gave her a friendly greeting, and she said, "Thank God that I found you so near."

"Lady, are you joking or were you looking for me?"

"Lord, if you don't mind, I was looking for you."

"What can I do for you?"

"You have long had to suffer hardships because of your own misdeeds as well as because of the disfavor of her who once made you ruler of this land and who now sends me to you. If she keeps her word, then I have managed things so that you will soon be my lord again as she is my mistress."

Both of them were happy, Sir Iwein more than he had ever been before. He kissed the lips, hands, and eyes of the girl a thousand times and said, "You truly have proven your regard for me. I fear and regret that my wealth or my life or both may not last long enough for me to reward you for your great friendship in a manner befitting the service you have done me." "Don't worry," she replied, "you will have plenty of wealth and years to show your kindness to me, if I have earned it, and to as many others as you wish. Even if you are well pleased, I have surely done no more for you than a debtor does who is ready to repay promptly what he has borrowed. You lent me a great deal when you saved me from being burned at the stake. You gave me back my life by risking your own: a thousand women wouldn't repay the debt I owe you." "Don't talk that way," he said. "You have greatly overpaid it. I have been rewarded a thousandfold for what I did for you. Now, tell me, Lady Lunete, does she know who I am?" "It would be too bad if she did," was the answer, "but, believe me, she knows only that you are the knight with the lion. She'll learn the rest in good time."

They met no one as they rode toward the castle and, through a strange bit of luck, reached Lunete's room without being seen. Then Lady Lunete went to her mistress, found her all alone at her prayers, and told her at once that the knight had come. She had never before heard news that pleased her so. "He is welcome," she said. "I would very much like to see him if it can be arranged properly. Go to him and find out whether he wants to come here or whether I should go there. I can go to him because I need him: if he needed me, he would have to come to me." Lady Lunete brought him very quickly, dressed in full armor, as she had directed, and her mistress received her husband as a stranger. At her first words of greeting he fell at her feet, but made no request. "Mistress," said Lady Lunete, "bid him stand up and then honor your oath, as I promised him you would, because, I assure you, the help he needs depends only on you."

"I'll do anything I can for him," replied her mistress. "Just tell me what." "Well spoken, lady," said the girl, "because no one could help him better. He is out of favor with his lady, but she will cease to be angry if you so command; if you do not, he is lost. That could cause you much grief, for truly you have no better friend than him. I found him so quickly because our Lord Jesus wished it and led me in the right direction so that, after a long separation, you two might be united again. From now on nothing should part you but death. So keep your promise and fulfill the oath: forgive his offense, because he has never loved and will never love any woman but you. This is Sir Iwein, your husband."

Dismayed at these words, the lady stepped back quickly and said, "If this is true, your trickery has simply handed me over to him. Should I spend the rest of my life with someone who cares nothing about me? I'd gladly forgo that. The storm never caused me such grief that I wouldn't rather endure it than give myself forever to a man who had no regard for me. I tell you truly that I wouldn't do it if it weren't for the oath. However, since it has trapped me, I'll forgive him and hope that this will earn me more affection than he has shown in the past." When Sir Iwein heard this and saw that the affair was turning out well, that his sorrow would end, he said, "Lady, I did wrong and am truly sorry. But one usually forgives the repentant sinner, however guilty he might be, as long as he makes amends by never offending thus again. This is all I ask because, if I win your good will, I shall never lose it again through any fault of mine." "I took an oath," she replied, "and can't take back my promise whether I like it or not." "This is the day," he said, "which I can indeed always call the Easter of my happiness."

"Sir Iwein, my dear lord," said the queen then, "be kind to me. I have caused you great suffering and ask you for God's sake to forgive me, since I shall regret it as long as I live." At this she fell at his feet and implored him earnestly. "Stand up," spoke the lord. "You are not to blame, for I lost your affection only through my own disposition." And thus they atoned for their offenses. It warmed Lady Lunete's heart to see them make their peace.

When man and wife have health, wealth, beauty, wit, youth, and no bad traits; and when these companions cherish each other; and when God lets them grow old; they win a great deal of happiness. That was to be expected here, and Lady Lunete, with her eagerness to serve, had helped bring it about. Through her cleverness she had so managed it that only good came out of the conflict between them, as she long had hoped. Her deeds surely deserved a reward, and I believe that she was so well paid that she never regretted the troubles she had had. One may suppose that a joyous life began at this court, but I don't know for certain what happened from this time on, since he from whom I got the story didn't say. So I can't tell you any more and shall only add: may God grant us His grace and the esteem of men!

Printed in the United States
96609LV00008B/1-24/A

9 780803 273313